Natalie
Parham.

Natalie
Parham

balloon. Mafaris.

Robert Kimmel Smith

jelly belly

Illustrated by Bob Jones

DELACORTE PRESS/NEW YORK

Published by
DELACORTE PRESS
1 Dag Hammarskjold Plaza
New York, N.Y. 10017

Text copyright © 1981 by Robert Kimmel Smith
Illustrations copyright © 1981 by Dell Publishing Co., Inc.

Manufactured in the United States of America

9 8 7 6 5

Library of Congress Cataloging in Publication Data

Smith, Robert Kimmel, 1930–
Jelly belly.

SUMMARY: The fattest kid in the fifth grade wants
to lose weight, but not badly enough to starve.
[1. Weight control—Fiction]   I. Jones, Bob, 1926–   II. Title.
PZ7.S65762Je   [Fic]   80–23898
ISBN 0–385–28477–2
ISBN 0–385–28479–9 lib. bdg.

*For the fat little boy who
grew up to be me*

1

I used to be the littlest one in my family until I grew.
Most kids grow up. I didn't. I grew out my front and
down my rear, in my chest and butt and especially in
my belly.

My name is Nathaniel Robbins. I'm four-feet-eight
inches tall, and I weigh one hundred and nine pounds.
My mother only weighs ninety-eight pounds.

Mom and the rest of the family call me "Ned." I got
that name because when I was a little kid I used to go
around either eating a piece of bread or asking for
bread, and that's the way I said bread, "Ned." My
friend Steve, who lives two houses down, calls me Nat.
The kids in school have a whole bunch of other names
for me.

Like Blimpie.

Tubby.

Piggy.

Lard-Butt.

1

And lots of others I wouldn't mention in public. But the one that gets me so mad I want to scream and spit and jump up and down on his head is the name that Phil Steinkraus gave me! "Jelly Belly."

Phil Steinkraus is this big kid who thinks he's so tough and so great he makes you want to vomit. Believe me, if you knew him like I do you'd feel the same way. In fact, Phil Steinkraus is so hateful, he made Steve and me stop taking the bus to school. We walk now, even if it's raining or snowing or freezing cold.

Because every day, when we walked down the aisle of the school bus and passed Phil Steinkraus, he'd do the same thing. "Hey, Jelly Belly," he'd say, and punch me in the stomach. Hard. "And Stevie Wonder," Phil'd say, and he'd punch Steve even harder.

That's why we don't ride the bus anymore.

Steve and me talked many times about ganging up on Phil Steinkraus and really beating him up. But we never did. And we never will. Because even if it was two against one, Phil Steinkraus would kill the both of us. He's about a whole head taller than me, and much bigger than Steve, too. But even more important, he's a whole lot meaner. I think he must like to punch people because he does it so often. I, on the other hand, am a very chicken kid.

Like when we're in the lunchroom sometimes, and I open my lunchbox and take out what Grandma has packed for me. Phil Steinkraus will come walking by, real easy like, and he'll look at my two sandwiches and my chocolate milk and my other goodies and he'll say something like "homemade doughnuts, my favorite," and he'll just take one of them without even asking. Bad enough, right? But not enough for Phil Steinkraus. Then he'll kind of give me that rotten grin of his and announce to the whole room, "What can shake but never break? *Jelly Belly!*"

Being the fattest kid in the fifth grade is not easy. And the nickname that Phil Steinkraus hung on me has stuck. Even Libby Klein, this very nice girl who lives around the corner and is in my class, even Libby calls me Jelly Belly once in a while. I guess she and the other kids figure that I don't mind that name too much. Or that I don't care.

I do care. It hurts me a lot.

Sometimes when I'm up on the top floor of our house, in the empty room, a place I go to when I want to be alone, or do some specially hard homework, or just to think, I look out on the trees and imagine how it would be if I was about twenty-five pounds skinnier.

I'd have to take in my belt about six notches, I bet. I wouldn't have all these double chins. I could look past my belly and see my feet without bending over. And best of all, I bet I could run a whole lot faster.

Being able to run faster is very important to me. Because I like to play baseball—love it, in fact—but when you're as slow as me you can't play all the positions. I wouldn't think of playing the outfield because I would never catch up to a really well-hit line drive. I can't play shortstop or second base because I don't have the range and speed you need there. And Mr.

Pezzino, the coach of the Hawks, the Little League team I play on, says that third base is out, too. I'm not quick enough. So I fill in sometimes at first base. But mostly, I'm the catcher.

I was playing catcher yesterday in a softball game in school.

It's May now, and on Friday afternoons we play these softball games, class against class, in the school-yard. It was one of those bright days, with the sun really beating down on the schoolyard pavement. About the fourth inning, my shirt was already soaking wet. (That's another thing about being overweight—you sweat more than normal people.)

Softball is fun, especially the way we play it in school with easy lob pitching. It means there's a lot of hitting and a lot of scoring. And a lot of crouching behind the plate during a lot of long innings.

Anyway, it was the ninth inning and we were a couple of runs behind. The score was something like 21 to 19.

I had doubled in a run in the third inning by socking one off the fence in left field, which most other kids would have had at least a triple on.

Steve led off our ninth by popping up to the short-stop. But then Libby Klein blooped one into right field for a hit. But Kevin Riley hit back to the pitcher —my friend and yours, Phil Steinkraus—and was thrown out at first.

That left it up to me. I stepped into the batter's box. If I could get on and score, we'd tie up the game.

4

Out on the mound, Phil Steinkraus was rubbing the ball and smiling that wolf grin of his. "Whaddya know, Jelly Belly," he called in to me. I didn't say anything. "C'mon, Tubby, let's see if you can hit it."

He threw up this high lob that if you swing and hit it, it would probably be a pop-up. I let it go by. And the next two pitches, too.

"Hey, Jelly Belly, you gonna stand there all day?" Phil Steinkraus yelled.

"Give me a good one," I yelled back.

Phil Steinkraus didn't say anything, but he did begin to throw them better.

I picked out a good pitch and swung as hard as I could. I could tell by the way it felt that I'd really hit that ball well. As I rounded first, I could see it bouncing off the wall in right field.

Libby was scoring and all the kids in the class were screaming. I rounded second base, running as hard and as fast as I could. But there is a great deal of difference in the way I run compared to most other kids in my class. In fact, if I was in a race with a one-legged turtle, I would say the turtle had a good chance at winning.

The relay was coming in from the outfield as I came to third base. "Run, Jelly Belly!" the kids were yelling as I turned for home. I couldn't see where the ball was, but I didn't care. I wanted a home run off Phil Steinkraus more than anything.

About halfway home, huffing and puffing, I saw

where the ball was. In the catcher's glove. Before I could stop running, I was tagged out.

And that was the ball game.

Libby Klein was standing behind home plate and she was furious. "You run like a hippo!" she yelled at me.

On the way home, I stopped off at the candy store on the corner near the school and bought a Milky Way. Even though I'm not supposed to eat candy anymore. And even though I'd promised my mom that I wouldn't have any after-school treats until I went away to camp in July. And even though Steve, who knows about my diet, told me not to buy it.

I wanted that Milky Way and I was going to have it.

I broke it in half and gave Steve the slightly smaller piece. We didn't say anything for a while as we walked home. I just sort of chewed and let that chocolatey taste roll around in my mouth.

"That was some shot you hit," Steve said.

"Yeah," I said.

"If I was running out that hit, I could have had a home run *and* a double."

"At least," I said.

"You tried," Steve said. "That's the main thing."

We crossed the street around the corner from home.

"Did you see how I was running?" I asked. "That's as fast as I can run."

"I know," Steve said. "But, Nat, it's really not too fast." And then Steve jabbed me on my arm, not hard, but friendly. "Kind of like a truck with one flat tire."

I smiled. "Like a huge Cadillac running on a little Volkswagen motor."

Steve laughed. "Faster than molasses."

"But not as fast as pancake syrup," I said.

And then we were both laughing, all the way home.

2

Let me tell you about my family.

My mother's name is Ruth, and she works for a textile company. She designs fabrics, and she's very artistic. Sometimes she brings work home to do, and she has her own drawing board in the den. We call the den her office.

My dad is a lawyer, but he always says "attorney." I usually do, too. He's not like one of those attorneys you see on TV, like Perry Mason, always getting involved with crooks and all that. He works for a big company in Manhattan, and mostly he does things like insurance and contracts. He's tall, about six-foot-four, but he's not very athletic. I mean, the last time he had a catch with me was maybe about five years ago. His name is Martin, and sometimes he brings work home, too.

My older brother, Jamie, is seventeen and very nice. He's tall, like my dad, plays the piano, and runs track for Wilson High School. Next year he'll be a senior. Jamie's room is on the top floor of our house and it's kind of private. The rest of us have rooms on the second floor, but Jamie likes it up there all alone. Mom fixed it up really neat, with this shaggy red rug on the floor, and plaid wallpaper. Except that Jamie has so many posters on the walls, you can hardly see the wallpaper anymore.

Jamie's okay, and sometimes we play Frisbee in the backyard.

The pill in our household is my older sister, Elizabeth. She thinks she's so great it makes you sick. I have to knock before I can go into her room, and she keeps the door closed. She's always going bonkers about some boy in school, and she likes to sit on the front porch whenever Michael—that's Steve's older brother —is home from college. Last year she got her own telephone, and like Jamie says, "We haven't seen her since." Elizabeth is built like my dad, too, long and stringy, sort of.

I, on the other hand, am built like Grandma.

Grandma is a terrific person, and probably one of the best cooks in the whole world. She came to live with us five years ago, when Grandpa died. She does all of the cooking for the family, except on weekends when Mom helps out. Come to think of it, the kitchen is Grandma's room. I mean, she's always hanging out there. Even at night, when I'm watching TV in the living room, Grandma's sitting in her chair at the kitchen table, sipping coffee and reading a newspaper.

Elizabeth gets mad at Grandma sometimes, especially when she comes home from a date with a boy and there's Grandma, sitting in the kitchen. What usually happens is Grandma has made some special cake or pie, and the boy ends up drinking milk and eating in the kitchen, talking to Grandma and ignoring Elizabeth.

Grandma says she doesn't stay up so late on purpose. She sleeps in the morning, after I've gone to school, but only for a couple of hours. She calls herself a night person.

The easiest one in the house to talk to is Grandma. I mean, she's so forgiving and understanding. Last year, when I broke her china cream pitcher, which was a gift Grandpa gave her on their twenty-fifth wedding anniversary and had their names on it, everyone in the whole house was mad at me but Grandma. "Leave the boy alone," she said, and she came over and mussed my hair and kissed me on the cheek. "You didn't drop it on purpose, did you, Neddie?" she asked. "Then why is everyone getting so excited?"

I can tell anything to Grandma and I know she won't criticize me. And she keeps secrets, too. Like when I told her about how scared I was of lightning and thunder, and she didn't make a joke out of it like Elizabeth did. So when there's a thunderstorm and I'm home, I go down to the kitchen and sit with Grandma. She gives me milk and cake and we sit and talk. And when there's a really close *ka-boom* of thunder, she just gives me a little look out of the corner of her eye and smiles. And I feel better.

10

Grandma is the only person in the house who doesn't think I'm too fat, either.

She and my parents are always getting into arguments about it. "Leave him alone, he's a growing boy," Grandma says. "When a child is hungry, you should let him eat."

"It's unhealthy," my mother says. "He's too heavy."

"I remember when you were his age," Grandma says. "What a little roly-poly you were."

"That's not the point," Mom says. "Ned has to diet."

"You grew out of it, didn't you? Neddie will do the same."

Lately, my parents seem to be winning the argument. Grandma only bakes three times a week now, instead of every day. On Mondays she makes doughnuts, enough to last for three or four days. Grandma's doughnuts are so good you don't have to have sugar or cinnamon on top. Wednesdays she makes a cake, usually a chocolate one because that's my favorite, and a couple of big rye breads. Fridays she bakes enough for the weekend. A big egg bread so delicious it tastes like cake. Two pies, apple with a flaky kind of crust, and another with whatever fruit is in season. And cookies. Wow, can she bake cookies! Round buttery ones with burnt edges, tan ones with sugar on top, applesauce cookies, peanut butter cookies, cookies with nuts or cherries in the middle, and of course, chocolate chip cookies.

Lucky for me, Mom and Dad have left for work by

the time I shove off for school. What's in my lunchbox is strictly between Grandma and me. Even though I'm supposed to be on a diet.

That diet. Yuch! A person could starve to death on that diet.

I'm supposed to eat only chicken, veal, and fish. No bread. And no cookies or cake or sweets of any kind. And lots of things like salad, which I hate, and tomato juice, which makes me want to throw up.

Take last night's dinner, for instance. We all sat down. On the table was a big loaf of Grandma's egg bread. As soon as I reached out to take a slice of it, Mom stopped me. "Neddie," she said, "not for you."

I looked at her.

"Your diet," she said, raising her eyebrows behind her glasses.

As if for spite, Elizabeth took a piece of egg bread and covered it all over with butter. She made sure I was looking at her and took a big bite.

"Just one slice?" I asked. I was so hungry my stomach was rumbling.

"Supper will be on the table in a minute," my Dad said. "Have a celery stalk."

That's another part of my diet. Celery stalks and sliced green peppers. I'm supposed to eat those instead of bread. I hate celery stalks. They taste like crunchy wet straw to me. But I was so starved I took one anyway. And when I took a bite, there was Lizzie, taking another bite of bread.

I guess Dad could read the look on my face, because

he reached out and touched my shoulder. "You may not like celery, Ned, but celery likes you. You know that every time you eat celery, your body burns up more calories consuming it than the celery actually contains? So you really lose weight just by eating it."

"Wonderful," I said in a funny way, and Jamie laughed.

"I don't think Neddie appreciates your explanation *or* the celery," he said.

Dad grinned. "I think you're right. Dieting is not easy. Especially for an eleven-year-old boy. But, Ned," he said, "you've got to stick with it. Lose some weight and you'll look better, you'll feel better, and what's more—you'll be a lot healthier, too."

"I feel healthy," I said.

"Well, you don't look healthy," Lizzie said. "You look . . . *gross*."

I shot her a look. Dad cleared his throat. "I think we could do without that sort of comment," he said to her.

"Just trying to help," Lizzie shrugged. "I mean, he is fat."

"Elizabeth," Mom said.

Just then Grandma began bringing food to the table. I took one look and got even hungrier. There were plates piled high with spaghetti and Grandma's special tomato sauce. And was that . . . yes! Breaded veal cutlets, my special favorite.

Mom helped Grandma serve, passing plates to everyone but me. Grandma sat down at her place across from me. I could see that she wasn't happy.

14

"And here's your dinner, Neddie," Mom said. She brought my plate to the table. There was no spaghetti on it, no tomato sauce, no breaded veal cutlet. Instead, there was this triangle of gray meat, a little pile of string beans, and a sliced tomato.

"No spaghetti?" I said.

"Sorry, hon," Mom said. "It's not on your diet."

"How about a veal cutlet?"

"That *is* a veal cutlet," Mom said.

"This thing?" I touched the gray thing with my fork.

"It's just not breaded and fried," Mom said. "It's broiled. Try it. I'm sure it's delicious."

I looked at Jamie mixing the tomato sauce through his pile of spaghetti and the smell made me go out of my mind. I wanted to reach over with my bare hands and stuff it all in my mouth.

Everyone at the table was staring at me, except Grandma.

"Come on, now," Dad said, "let's eat." Jamie twirled his fork around and picked up a bunch of spaghetti. Elizabeth was already stuffing her mouth.

I wanted to cry, but I didn't. I sat there, staring at my plate, trying not to look at what everyone else was eating. After a while, I cut a piece of the gray meat and put it in my mouth. It tasted just the way it looked. Like gray meat.

But if that was all I was going to get for dinner, I had to eat it. I was just about as hungry as I've ever been, but deep down inside there was another feeling, too. A kind of sad feeling that made it hard to swallow.

I ate everything on my plate without looking up.

15

"Ruth," Grandma said, "this is wrong."

"Not now, Mother," Mom said in the tight voice she uses when she's angry.

"Neddie will just have to get used to it," Dad said to Grandma. "We can't all stop eating because Ned has to diet."

"I could serve him first," Grandma said. "Or he could eat in the dining room."

"Nonsense," Dad said. "We're a family. We eat together."

"It's still wrong," Grandma said. I could see that she hadn't even touched the food on her plate. Now she stood up from the table and walked out of the kitchen.

In a little while, Mom cleared the table. Then she came back, wheeling the serving cart. On the cart were a bunch of plates, a pitcher of milk, and my absolute favorite dessert: one of Grandma's blueberry pies.

I looked at the pie and I looked at my mom. "I'm sorry, Neddie," she said.

There wasn't going to be any pie for me. Not now, and maybe not forever.

I wiped my mouth with my napkin, put it on the table, and walked quietly out of the kitchen and up to my room.

Only after I closed the door did I let myself start crying.

3

Right now there are probably three million kids reading this and laughing at me. I mean, you're probably saying, "Big deal—the kid misses one meal of spaghetti and a piece of blueberry pie and he runs upstairs and cries his head off."

But it wasn't really that at all.

I was lying there across my bed, miserable and crying, because there wasn't any answer to it all. I was *always* going to be fat, I was *always* going to be on a stupid diet, and I was *always* going to be miserable.

It just seemed like there was no hope. It was going to be the way it was, forever and ever. And that's why I was crying.

I could take a diet for a week or a month. But the fact was I had already been on a diet for four months and *I hadn't lost any weight*.

The diet started at Dr. Brandt's office, when I went for my annual checkup. Dr. Brandt is okay, even nice, in fact. And he knew me since I was a baby. He didn't seem to care in the last few years when I began to put on weight. I mean, he never said much about it at all. But this last time we went there, my mom brought it up. "Isn't he a little overweight?" she asked Dr. Brandt.

"About twenty-five pounds, yes."

"Don't you think Nathaniel should be on a diet?" Mom said.

Dr. Brandt looked at me and smiled. "Yes, I think he could knock off some weight. I'll give you a diet for him, if you like."

I wasn't always fat. In fact, until I was six I was a really skinny kid. When we went to the beach in the summer, Dad always counted my ribs and tickled me. All my ribs used to stick out then. But I began to eat better, and I stopped growing so fast, and little by little my shape started to change.

I was just about right when I was seven. A little chunky when I was eight. I had a bit of a belly when I was nine. By ten my butt started to stick out. And in the last year, Jelly Belly.

Mom came into my room later and we sat on my bed and talked for a while. She looked about as sad as me. She hugged me and pushed the hair back out of my eyes like she sometimes does. "Neddie," she said, "I want you to know this. I love you the same way now as I did when you were skinny. And if you never lose a pound, I'll still love you. Do you understand?"

I nodded.

"But honey, we've got to help you lose weight. All of us in this house, including Grandma. It's not healthy, walking around with all those extra pounds on you, Neddie."

"I know."

"You want to lose weight, don't you?"

"Sure I do. But this diet . . . I get hungry, Mom."

"I know," Mom nodded. "You'll have to learn to control it, honey."

"And when I see people eating things I love . . . like tonight . . ."

"Then it's extra hard," Mom said.

"Not extra hard. Mom, it's impossible!"

She laughed and squeezed me again, then we went downstairs. Dad was sitting at the kitchen table with his reading glasses on. He had a color brochure in his hands and was looking through it.

And that was the first time I heard about Camp Lean-Too.

4

The more they told me about Camp Lean-Too, the more I knew I was going to hate it. Imagine a camp for kids where the whole idea is to make them lose weight. No one had to tell me how a camp would do that. They would starve everybody, that's how.

It was a rotten idea and unfair, besides. For the past three summers I had gone away to Camp Sha-Kan-Ah-Kee with Steve Adolphus. The first year I hadn't liked it so much, but the last two summers were great. Steve and I were in the same bunk, and we'd made some good friends. I knew every inch of Camp Sha-Kan-Ah-Kee like I knew my own room. There was a big blue lake back beyond the ball field, good tennis and basketball courts, and evening baseball leagues five nights a week. And the food was terrific.

"You're going to love it up there at Camp Lean-Too," Dad was saying. "I just know it."

"I don't want to go," I said.

Mom and Dad exchanged one of those glances of theirs. "Look at it this way," Mom said. "It's a chance to spend two months away *and* lose a lot of weight."

"You could be slim and trim when you come back, Ned," Dad said.

"But I like Camp Sha-Kah-Na-Kee."

"They have an Olympic-size swimming pool," Dad said. He showed me the picture in the brochure.

"Sha-Kah-Na-Kee has a great lake," I said.

"Tennis courts, arts and crafts, and a riding stable," Dad said.

"I hate horses."

"You're going to love it," Mom said. "Just give it a chance."

I didn't know it right then, but that was the beginning of a family campaign. And the advertising slogan was "You're going to love it at Camp Lean-Too."

I, on the other hand, knew I was going to hate it.

The scary part was what the brochure called their "carefully supervised dietary program that guarantees weight loss." Oh, boy! When you put that into English, it means they probably don't feed you anything, and what they do give you to eat, stinks.

I wasn't kidding when I said the food at Camp Sha-Kah-Na-Kee is great. You can have a hamburger for lunch any time you want, with potato chips. They have a real neat canteen, where you can buy a candy bar every day—they even have ice cream sundaes. And when your bunk wins an award for something, the counselors take you into town for a pizza party.

Even their bug juice doesn't taste too bad. Camp Lean-Too. To me it sounded like a cabin in the woods where all there is to eat is grass.

But I was going there, like it or not. Dad had already sent a deposit. And every single day either Mom or Dad was sure to say "You're going to love it at Camp Lean-Too."

For the next few weeks before camp I was really low. Camp Lean-Too scared me. It sounded like a jail for fat kids. Like some judge had said, "I sentence you, Nathaniel Robbins, to sixty days hard labor in Camp Lean-Too, where you shall have nothing to eat but bread and water."

Probably they wouldn't even have bread.

The one who was a big help to me during those awful weeks before camp was Jamie. I was lucky to have a big brother like him. One thing about Jamie, he's always honest. He tells you what he thinks all the time, and you can speak to him the same way.

We were up in his room on the third floor, listening to one of his new records. Jamie has this bright red beanbag chair I like, and I was kind of curled up on it. "It's scary, Jamie," I was saying. "It's going to be a rotten camp. I know *it*."

"Probably," Jamie said. He was stretched out on his back on the rug. "But look at it this way, Ned—it's only a couple of months. And if you're lucky, you'll probably lose some weight."

"Knowing me," I said, "I'll probably be the only kid who comes back weighing more than when he went up there."

Jamie smiled. "You do want to lose weight, don't you?"

"Sure I do. I mean, I guess I do," I said. "I don't know."

"Pick one of the above," Jamie grinned.

"I want to lose weight," I said. "Really."

"But you don't want to enough," Jamie said.

"Right."

"I understand," Jamie said. He put his hands behind his head and began to do leg raises. "I would like to be number one on the cross-country team next year," he said, "but I won't be. For the same reason. I don't want to enough."

"But you're a very good runner," I said. Jamie had finished his second year on the track team at Wilson High. The two-mile was his best event, but he also ran cross-country.

"Not as good as Lynn or Covelli," Jamie said. "They work at it."

"You work at it, too."

"Not really," Jamie said. "Not like I should. I'm like you, Neddie. I want to be number one cross-country like you want to lose weight. But we're not working at it."

Jamie was staring at me and I looked away from his honest blue eyes. He was right about me. I didn't want to lose weight enough. Not really. Or else I would stop doing what I was doing, which was stuffing my face when I got the chance. And not resisting those sudden urges.

For a moment I considered telling Jamie about

those urges. But I couldn't. It was secret, something I couldn't tell anyone.

Like the stash of candy I had down in my room, hidden away in the locked drawer in my desk.

The secret trips to the pizza parlor on the way home from school sometimes, or in the evening when I was supposed to be going to Steve's house.

I couldn't confess to my middle-of-the-night visits to the kitchen, after Grandma had gone to bed. And all the secret pieces of cake I'd eaten, the stolen cookies, the bowls of ice cream I'd gobbled down, carefully washing the dish and putting it away so no one would ever know.

That's why my diet would not work. Because I was secretly snacking and nibbling and undermining the whole idea. I wanted to lose weight, all right. But I didn't want it enough.

Jamie grinned at me and did his very good imitation of Dad's voice. "You're going to love it at Camp Lean-Too," he said.

5

The morning I was to go away to camp I woke up with that scared feeling in the bottom of my stomach. Like in September, before the first day of school. After I'd finished dressing and washing up, Dad came into the bathroom. "Jump on the scale, Ned," he said. "I'd like to see what you weigh before you go off to camp."

"But I'm all dressed," I said.

He looked at me.

"I never weigh myself when I'm all dressed," I said. (You bet I didn't. With sneakers, socks, jeans, and a shirt on I weighed about three pounds more than when I was naked.)

"We'll weigh you dressed the same way when you come back," Dad said. He looked down at the scale and then at me. Without saying anything he crouched down and turned the little wheel that made the numbers on the scale move.

"Don't do that," I said.

"The pointer was about four pounds below zero," Dad said. "I'm fixing it."

"But it's always like that," I said, which was a big fat lie. Sometimes I turned the wheel so the scale showed ten pounds below zero. It felt terrific to weigh less, even if I did it just by turning a wheel.

I got on the scale, making sure that the tips of my sneakers kind of leaned over the front end. You weigh about two pounds less that way.

Dad leaned down to read the scale. "One hundred and sixteen pounds," he said. "I can't believe it."

"Well, sure," I grumbled, "if you're going to weigh me all dressed and push the numbers forward . . ."

"Let's have breakfast," Dad said.

Grandma was at the stove when we came downstairs. She kissed the top of my head and gave me a squeeze. "Just for you, a special treat," she said. "Because you're going away."

I could smell what it was before she said it. Orange French toast! Grandma takes some of her egg bread, soaks it in eggs and milk, and puts in orange juice and some of the rind of the orange. I love it.

She made me three big pieces and put the sugar bowl down in front of me. I saw her give my mom a look, as if to say "Stay out of this."

I ate slowly, tasting every mouthful, and trying to make the good taste last. Dad looked up from reading the paper and frowned. "I think some people will kill you with kindness," he said.

"Some people don't understand anything," Grandma said. "What do you think, a boy is going to be away a whole summer and I shouldn't give him something to remember?" She was kissing the top of my head again.

Dad sighed. "A hundred and sixteen pounds," he said.

The bus wasn't coming until later in the morning, so there was some time after breakfast. I was up in my room, putting my baseball glove and an old tennis ball that had lost its fuzz into my little overnight bag, when Grandma came in. She closed the door behind her, which she never does. She had a package, a shoebox. "Is there room in your bag for this?" she asked.

"What's in it?"

"Something you love, for when you get lonely."

I took a peek inside. Everything was wrapped in aluminum foil.

"Don't open them now," Grandma said. "I made chocolate chip cookies, some sugar ones, and a lot of peanut butter cookies, because they don't get stale so fast."

I gave her a hug. "You're the best grandma in the whole wide world," I said.

Grandma kissed me. "Do your best, Neddie," she said. "And share with the other kids, okay? And I'm not going with you to the bus because I'll probably start crying. And if I were you, I wouldn't tell Mom and Dad about what I just gave you. Let it be our secret."

I tucked the shoebox deep into my bag and covered

it with my St. Louis Cardinal's T-shirt. I've been a Cardinal fan ever since I got Ted Simmons's autograph three years ago.

It was time to leave for the bus, and we drove over to the pickup point, which was a parking lot about a half hour from our house. I have to tell you that I was very quiet during the ride in the car, because I had this sticking feeling in my throat, like pins and needles.

The bus was waiting when we got there, and a pretty good crowd, too. Lots of parents, and brothers and sisters, and some counselors and staff members from camp. They were the ones wearing the Camp Lean-Too T-shirts.

After a while, one of the staff blew a whistle and kids started getting on the bus.

"Have a wonderful time," Mom said. She kissed me and gave me a squeeze. "And write at least a couple of times a week."

"I will," I said. My voice sounded funny to me.

Dad hugged me. "So long, Neddie," he said. "Do what they tell you, and be good." I leaned up and kissed him, which I know he likes me to do.

I started up the steps to the bus and I felt about as low as an ant's toenail. I remembered the first time I went off to camp, four years ago. That was scary, too, but not as bad as now. Back then I was holding Steve's hand, and we sat together all the way up to Camp Sha-Kah-Na-Kee. Now I was heading off to a place I'd never been, on a bus full of strangers, going to a camp where they'd probably starve me to death.

6

There was this big fat kid sitting next to me on the bus, Richard Napoli. He was so huge I hardly had room on the seat. In a way, sitting next to him was good, because this was going to be his second summer at Camp Lean-Too. He said the camp stinks, but it wasn't too bad, which made me feel a little better.

All the way up to camp, Richard kept sticking his hand in his travel bag and putting things in his mouth. I mean he ate from the beginning of the trip until the end. Cookies, candy bars, two sandwiches, and about a zillion cherries. "You're bringing stuff up to camp?" he asked me between mouthfuls. I told him I was, thinking of my secret Grandma stash. "You better eat it now," Richard said.

I told him I'd wait awhile and save it, and Richard laughed.

A little while later, when we arrived in Camp Lean-Too and got off the bus, I knew why he laughed. Because the first thing the staff did was take us into the rec hall along with our travel bags. Then we had to empty our bags in front of us on the floor. Two counselors came around and took away my shoebox full of Grandma's cookies, and all the other goodies from the rest of the kids. (When they looked at Richard's stuff, all they took away was an empty paper bag.) It was disgusting. I mean, it was bad enough that they took away my cookies, but the way they did it was terrible. They were laughing and joking and making smart remarks.

I, on the other hand, didn't think that stealing a person's private property was funny at all.

When we marched out of the rec hall to go to a meeting, I got a good look at all the kids assembled in one bunch. It was frightening. I know I do not look like your average eleven-year-old kid. Not with my belly and butt. But I looked like Joe Skinny next to some of them. There was one older boy who could be a fat man in a circus. He was so huge he almost couldn't walk. And there was a girl wearing shorts, with skinny legs and an upper body so big you wondered how those little legs could hold it up.

I was going to a camp with a bunch of freaks!

The meeting was held across from the dining hall, under a bunch of trees. We all sat on the ground and there was this platform down front that the staff sat on. I stuck with Richard because he was the only one I knew. Richard knew a lot of the other kids and most of the older staff. After we got greetings from some lady

(Gertie, the nurse, Richard said), a tall man got up and introduced himself. Dr. Skinner, he said his name was, but Richard whispered in my ear that everyone called him Dr. Skinny. He wasn't a real doctor, according to Richard, but a dietician.

"We are here to reeducate you about food," Dr. Skinner was saying. "And the first thing I want to tell you is to forget about food. You think about food much too much. So get it right out of your mind."

Forget about food? You know what jumped into my head when he said that? It was getting to be time for lunch and I was hungry.

"Food has become a crutch that you lean on as you walk through the road of life," Dr. Skinner said. "When you are sad, you turn to food to cheer you up. When you are happy, you eat something to celebrate. When you are bored, you eat just to have something to do. Well, you are not going to think about food all the time at Camp Lean-Too."

"Is he kidding?" Richard said under his breath, and a couple of kids around us laughed.

"I want you to throw yourself into camp activities," Dr. Skinner went on. "Sports help take your mind off food and give you healthy exercise. Swimming, running, basketball, baseball, soccer, and tennis will help you thin down. Go at them vigorously, play hard, and you will lose weight."

From the dining hall across the way, a disgusting odor was drifting into my nostrils. "Oh, God," Richard said.

"What is that terrible smell?" I whispered.

"Lunch."

It was some kind of unidentified fish. When we sat down in the dining room they put it in front of me and I could hardly bear to look at it, let alone eat it. On the plate with the fish was some kind of vegetable I'd never seen before. It looked like pale green marbles, and tasted awful. Richard told me it was Brussels sprouts.

"They're very big on Brussels sprouts up here," Richard said. "Ignore them."

I could ignore the sprouts, but the fish was something else. I've had fish before, and I like it. Grandma makes fried fish with a crunchy breading that's not too bad. But this fish was naked, staring up at me all pale and white. There were a few raw carrot strips on the plate and I ate all of them. On the table, which seated about ten campers, there was absolutely nothing else. No salt, no pepper, no water, no milk, and especially no bread.

"Is this all we're getting for lunch?" I asked Richard.

"We get milk and dessert, too," he said.

"Dessert?"

"Don't get excited," he grinned. "A piece of fruit."

I was hungry, very hungry, and if this was all there was for lunch I had to eat it. I tried. The fish was white and milky when I broke it up with my fork. It didn't look very good and it tasted the same way. I had a few bites of it. Then I tried another Brussels sprout. It still tasted terrible, like cauliflower or cabbage, two of the vegetables I never eat. I pushed it aside.

"If you're not going to eat your fish," the kid on my right said, "I'll have it." He was about my age, it looked like, and very serious looking. He had these braces on his teeth and he wore horn-rim glasses with thick lenses. He ate the rest of my fish and had all the sprouts, too.

Richard introduced me to the kid who finished my lunch. He called him "Hog." His real name was Darryl Hawkins and, like me, he was going into the fifth grade in the fall. He'd been here last summer with Richard.

"I lost seventeen pounds last year," Hog Hawkins said. "And I gained twenty-five back over the winter. My parents are going to give me a dollar for every pound I lose up here."

"You won't make very much," Richard said.

A waiter came and put glasses of what looked like milk in front of us. It was thin and watery, and sort of blue. It was skim milk. "I hate skim milk," I said.

"Get used to it," Hog said. "That's the only kind of milk they serve."

I gagged a little, but I managed to drink it. On the way out of the dining hall we picked up dessert. One teeny-tiny apricot. I chewed it up in two bites. I was still so hungry I even thought about eating the pit.

After lunch we were all assigned bunks. If you've never been to camp, let me tell you what a bunk is. It's a kind of a little cabin, or hut, where you sleep and keep all your stuff. We had neat bunks in Camp Sha-Kah-Na-Kee, with lots of room to spread out. The bunk in Camp Lean-Too was much smaller, and the beds were double-deckers, but it wasn't too bad. There were two toilets in a small room, then another room with two sinks and a stall shower.

It looked like I was going to be lucky, at least for friends. Richard Napoli and Hog Hawkins were both in my bunk, along with three other kids. As soon as we got into our bunk, Richard tossed his travel bag onto a lower bunk. I took the lower one next to his, and Hog took the one right over me.

In a little while this tall, skinny guy came into the bunk. "Hello, everyone," he said. "My name is Gregg and I'm your counselor for the summer." He had a nice smile and he came over to me and shook hands. He looked just a little older than Jamie.

Gregg introduced everyone to everyone. The kid who took the upper bunk above Richard was named Max Cohen, and he came from Chicago. He was a year older than me and he was at Lean-Too to lose twenty pounds over the summer. He had a name for what we ate for lunch that I'd never heard before, and I don't think I ought to write it down here because it's probably not too nice.

The other two kids in the bunk were friends and it was their first time at Camp Lean-Too, too. Their names were Fred Mastric and Brian Hume. They were both from Long Island.

All of our camp trunks were already in the bunk, and with Gregg helping we shoved them around until they were near our beds. "Now then," Gregg said, "it's inspection time. I want you to open your trunks and take everything out and put it on your bunks." He looked at Richard and smiled. "Not that I don't trust you not to bring food up here . . . but let's be sure."

Hog Hawkins groaned, kind of low so Gregg couldn't hear. We all began emptying our stuff onto the beds.

There were forty-eight Almond Joy bars in Hog's trunk, stuffed down on the bottom under his blankets. Gregg took them and put them into a big plastic trash bag. "That's very dumb," Gregg said. "You're up here to lose weight, Hawkins, not to eat candy all summer."

There were five cans of peanuts, two bags of pretzels, and a carton of Hershey bars in Max Cohen's trunk.

Fred Mastric lost six one-pound packages of M&M's.

Brian Hume lost a box of pretzels, six Chunky bars, and what looked like a huge salami to Gregg's plastic trash bag.

Only Richard's trunk and mine were clean.

"Boys, boys," Gregg was saying, shaking his head. "I see I'll have to watch you guys closely all summer." He picked up the trash bag and headed for the door. "General swim for everyone in one hour. I'll be back."

We all started moaning and groaning, except Richard. "I think you guys need to have a nibble, right?"

We all looked at him. Richard went to his trunk and took out one of his six cans of tennis balls. He took off the plastic cover, rolled out the tennis ball on top, and showed me what was in the rest of the can.

Corn chips.

"It's a good thing one of us is smart," he said, "or we'd starve to death this summer."

7

The next day, *after lunch,* I had a meeting with Dr. Skinny and a weigh-in. Talk about unfair, imagine weighing somebody right after lunch.

I never weigh myself at home after lunch. Because I know that after lunch is probably the fattest time of the day. Naturally, Dr. Skinny weighed me in my jeans, sneakers, and shirt. I wasn't surprised when the scale said I weighed 118.

"Let's talk awhile about your program for the summer, shall we?" Dr. Skinny said. He was one of those people who moves his head around when he speaks, kind of telling you what he wants you to say. He nodded when he wanted you to say yes, and he shook his head from side to side when he wanted you to say no.

I sat down in the straight chair by Dr. Skinny's desk.

"Now then," he said, "according to my chart, your proper weight for your height would be seventy-five pounds. You do know that you are grossly overweight, don't you?" Nod-nod went his head.

"Yes."

"And you do want to lose weight, don't you?" Nod-nod.

"Yes."

Dr. Skinny smiled. He seemed happy with my answers so far.

"Now then, you are forty-three pounds overweight. You are going to be with us for eight weeks. I think a realistic goal for you, Nathaniel, would be a weight loss of twenty pounds." Nod-nod.

"Sounds good," I said.

"You don't think twenty pounds is too high?" Shake-shake.

"No."

"Very good. I'm glad you're so cooperative. Are you happy up here so far?" Nod-nod.

"Yes."

"I'm sure of it. We do take your mind off food, don't we?" Nod-nod.

"Yes," I said, which was maybe the biggest lie of my life. I hardly thought about anything else but food up there.

"Good." Dr. Skinny stood up and I did, too. He walked me to the door. "See you next week for your weigh-in," he said. He shook my hand. "You won't be too unhappy if you lose *more* than twenty pounds, will you?" Shake-shake.

"Not at all."

Dr. Skinny was very happy. "Good-bye, Nathaniel."

"Good-bye, Doctor."

Talking with Dr. Skinny was like taking a test in school with someone giving you all the answers.

8

One day the menu outside the dining room said we were going to have hamburgers for lunch. I didn't get too excited. By now I knew that Camp Lean-Too's idea of a certain food was a lot different than mine.

"What's the hamburger like up here?" I asked Richard.

"What do you think?"

"Terrible."

"You got it," Richard said.

Now, my idea of a hamburger is something like this. First of all, a nice bun. Not too fat and not too thin, and toasted. Next, the burger has to be juicy, but not too rare. Kind of medium. Then I need to have ketchup on it. A lot. And if there were some fried onions to put on top, that'd be okay, too. And there would be french fries, of course, or potato chips, and a chocolate milkshake goes best, but I could also take a Coke to wash it down.

Here is Camp Lean-Too's idea of a hamburger. A thin round gray hamburger on a plate.

That's it. No ketchup, no bun, no onions, no french fries, no milkshake, no Coke. The only thing they serve it with is a scoop of cottage cheese.

"This is getting serious," Hog was saying. We were hanging around the bunk, having an after-lunch snack. "A person could starve up here."

What we were snacking on was the stash hidden in a couple of Richard's tennis ball cans. M&M's and pretzels. They make a terrific combination.

"We have to get into town," Richard said. "My stuff isn't going to last us very long. Not the way you guys eat."

"How do you get into town?" Max Cohen asked.

"There are ways," Richard said. "I'm thinking about it."

"You better figure it out before I die of starvation," Hog said.

"There's one big problem," said Richard. "Gregg."

"Wait a minute," I said. "Gregg is okay. He's nice."

Richard looked at me like I was stupid. "Yeah, yeah, he's nice all right. Nice and honest, that's the trouble."

I didn't really understand what Richard meant by Gregg being too honest, but I didn't say anything.

"How about we raid the kitchen?" Max said.

"That's an idea," Hog agreed.

"There's got to be something to eat in there," Max said. "I mean . . . it's a kitchen, isn't it?"

Richard thought about that for a minute or two.

"Okay," he shrugged, "we can try it. When we go to dinner tonight, let's scout around. Then we'll make a plan."

If anybody had been watching us at dinner that night, we would have looked highly suspicious. Because we were concentrating more on seeing into the kitchen through the swinging doors than we were on eating our food.

Considering what the food was, we didn't miss anything.

After dinner, we walked around the dining hall to the back, where we could look into the kitchen. There was a back door with a screen door on it, and a couple of windows.

"No problem," Richard said, when we had gathered back at the bunk. "We wait until everyone goes to sleep, then we make our move. Hog and Max will be lookouts. Ned and me will go inside."

"What if the door is locked?" I asked.

"It won't be," said Richard.

I looked at him for a moment. To tell you the truth, I wasn't so sure I wanted to break into the kitchen. I mean, it would be like stealing, and I had never done that.

"You guys are crazy," Brian Hume, one of the Long Island kids, said. Brian and Fred sort of went their own way. After the first time they shared some of Richard's goodies, they hadn't had anymore.

"Maybe they're right," I said.

"And maybe you're chicken," Richard said. He tapped me on the arm. "It'll be all right. Trust me."

44

I didn't say anything.

"Don't you raid the kitchen at home sometimes?" Richard asked. How did he know that? Nobody in my whole family knew that. "Sometimes," I said.

"We all do it," Richard said. "So just make believe that you're raiding your own kitchen at home. And if we get caught, the most they'll do is yell at us. Just like at home."

"What else could they do?" Hog said. "Take away our treats?"

We played a softball game in our after-dinner league that night. I haven't told you anything about our sports activities because they are very hard to describe. You see, we didn't have any normal-sized kids on the field. Everyone was too fat, nobody could run fast, and most of the kids had trouble bending down to pick up a grounder. I, on the other hand, was one of the better ball players because I wasn't as huge as some of them. I played shortstop. And I liked it.

After showers, we lay on our beds, planning the raid and worrying a lot. Nobody put on pajamas, because Richard said it would look ridiculous to get caught raiding the kitchen while wearing pajamas. So we were pretending we were going to sleep in our underwear. Later on, after Gregg's bed check, we'd get dressed.

It takes a long time to get dark when you're just waiting for it to. Longer than you'd think.

We climbed into bed at lights out, said good night to Gregg, and talked quietly in the dark. We knew Gregg always came back about an hour after lights out to check if we were okay. We heard him come up the front steps of the bunk and open the screen door. I think I saw his flashlight shine on my face, but I couldn't tell for sure because I had my eyes shut. After a minute, he went away.

We waited a little while to make sure Gregg was gone, then we got out of bed and dressed. In spite of what Richard and Hog had said, I was still scared.

"No talking when we get outside," Richard whispered to us. "Just follow me and be quiet." He opened the screen door of the bunk and tiptoed out. Max and Hog followed, and I went out last and closed the door very gently. We stepped off the porch and started sneaking down the line of bunks that led to the dining room. At the end of the row there was a big clear space leading to the basketball courts and the assembly area. There was a kind of street light shining, and two older counselors were shooting baskets. Richard held up a hand to stop us before we crossed into the light. "Follow me," he whispered, and he turned around so we could circle through the trees and avoid the lighted place.

It was spooky in among the trees in the pitch dark. You felt like something was going to jump out from behind a tree and grab you. Also, we kept bumping into things. Bushes, branches, and sometimes each other.

It took a long time, but we finally got to the edge of the trees behind the kitchen end of the dining room. There was a grassy space about as big as a baseball diamond to cross. A half-moon hung in the sky, just over the trees, and it gave a kind of silvery light that made the grass shine.

We rested awhile, looking across the grass at the kitchen door. I'm not ashamed to say that my heart was hammering in my chest, and my mouth felt very dry.

"Maybe we shouldn't do this," Max said, very low.

"Exactly what I was thinking," I said.

"Don't be chicken," Richard said. "I'll lead. Ned, you follow me. Max and Hog, you guys walk after us and go to the edge of the building, so you can peek around the corner. If you see anybody coming around to the back, hoot like an owl so we can hear you inside."

"How do you hoot like an owl?" Hog whispered.

"Just do it," Richard said. "Let's go." And with that, he set off across the grass, walking like it was bright daylight and he was out for a stroll. I followed him, with Max and Hog coming behind me.

Richard was waiting at the back door of the kitchen. He opened the screen door very slowly, then put his hand on the doorknob and pushed open the kitchen door. I followed him inside.

We stood together just inside the door, trying to see in the blackness. After a minute, we could make out the big tables in the center of the room, the line of stoves, the whole wall of refrigerators. We went across the room to the big refrigerators. When Richard opened the first one and the light came on I almost jumped out of my sneakers. We looked inside to-gether. There was about a ton of margarine and butter in there, and nothing else. "Great," Richard said. He closed the first refrigerator and moved to the next one in line. It was filled with these great big tubs of cottage cheese. In the next refrigerator we found nothing but gallons and gallons of skim milk.

The next three refrigerators turned out to be freezers. They were filled with frozen meat and fish and vegetables. "Not even one rotten pint of ice cream," Richard whispered. He moved down the line and I followed. It was the last refrigerator, and it was filled with packages of American cheese. Richard reached in and took two packages and told me to do the same. "I don't like American cheese," I whispered. Richard took two more packages and put them on the long table in the center of the room.

There was a little room in the corner of the kitchen, and I followed Richard to it. It was something like a big closet, and we walked inside. There was a string hanging down that turned on a light on the ceiling, and after I closed the door behind us, Richard switched it on. It was kind of a pantry, with shelves leading up almost to the ceiling. There were cans and cans of soups, vegetables, tomato sauce, and tuna fish. One whole shelf held nothing but low calorie imitation mayonnaise. "No nuts, no chips, no pretzels," Richard said. "Beautiful!" Back in the kitchen, we scouted around. I found a kind of bin where they kept the bread. I took a long loaf of sliced white bread, Richard picked up the packages of cheese, and we tiptoed out the back door. Max and Hog came running.

48

"What d'ya get?" Hog whispered.

"Not now," Richard said. "Come on."

We sneaked back to the bunk the way we came. Then we went into the bathroom and put on the light. Hog and Max looked at our loot. Richard started ripping open the packages of cheese while I unwrapped the bread.

"American cheese!" Hog said. "I never eat American cheese. Except maybe a grilled cheese sandwich, with bacon."

Richard began making cheese sandwiches. And I got some paper cups and filled them with water from the sink.

"The only way I like a cheese sandwich is with lettuce, tomato, butter, and about a ton of mayonnaise," Max said.

Richard handed out the sandwiches. "Shut up and eat," he said.

9

One of the few good things about being in this camp was getting mail from home. It's a funny thing about letters you get from your family. They cheer you up, but at the same time they make you a little lonely. I guess because they remind you of the people you miss.

Dear Ned:

Received your letter this afternoon and I'm answering immediately as you requested. I'm glad to hear you've made friends up at Camp Lean-Too. I'm sorry to hear that you think the food is terrible. Perhaps it will improve. And if it doesn't, just remember that eating less will help you lose weight. (Ha! Ha!)

I'm looking forward to seeing you on Visiting Day. Things are very calm and peaceful at home, and you're not missing anything. Except that we all miss you.

Love,
Dad

My father probably doesn't know it, but in every letter he sends me he says that things are peaceful at home and I'm not missing anything. I'd still rather be there than here.

Dear Neddie:

We are all looking forward to seeing you on Visiting Day. Grandma wants to bake everything you like, but we keep getting these instructions from camp telling us that if we bring up food it will be taken away.

I know you want your goodies, honey, but a rule is a rule. It doesn't mean we love you any less if we don't bring up cakes and doughnuts. I'm telling you now that we won't. We'll bring just us, to see the boy we love. Please try to understand, Neddie.

I can't wait to meet your new friend, Richard. From what you say, he sounds like a lovely boy.

Dr. Skinner wrote (we get a weekly report) that you have lost two pounds in the first three weeks in camp. Don't be disappointed at your slow progress. We are not. You'll probably lose more in the second half of camp.

See you soon.

Hugs and kisses,
Mom

Well, that was the answer I expected when I asked for some goodies from home on Visiting Day. I knew it wouldn't do any good. You see, Richard and Hog told me about what they did last year. The camp staff did

51

take away all the goodies that the parents brought up. *But not until the parents had gone home!*

Which means that for a few hours at least I could have had some of Grandma's home cooking. But my mom and dad are great ones for listening to rules.

My dear sweet lovely Neddie:

I got your nice letter the other day and I was thrilled to hear from you . . . I even kissed the letter—which I hope you don't tell to anybody because only a crazy grandmother like me would do such a thing. I'm sure they are not feeding you good, darling, who could know what you like but me? I am having a big fight with your mother about Visiting Day which you must know by now. Here I was, planning to bring you so many things like I always do every year and she is telling me I can't. It is breaking my heart not to bake for you, that's the truth, but a mother is the boss and not a grandma, no matter how much it hurts. I miss you every day and I can't wait to kiss your sweet face.

Your Grandma

10

"Come in, Nathaniel," said Dr. Skinny, "and get on the scale."

It was after lunch, of course. And one of the few good lunches they served at Camp Lean-Too. Hog called it "naked" chicken. That's because they took all the skin off the chicken, put some kind of tomato sauce on top, and they served it with mashed carrots. When you swished some of the tomato sauce through the carrots it didn't taste too bad. In fact, it was one of the few lunches where I didn't leave any leftovers for Hog to finish.

"Hmmm," said Dr. Skinny, looking at the scale. "One fifteen. That's not very good, Nathaniel, is it?" Shake-shake.

"No, sir."

"A three-pound weight loss after three weeks. I would call that disappointing, wouldn't you?" Nod-nod.

"Yes, I would."

"Sit down, and let's have a little talk." Dr. Skinny got these deep wavy lines across his forehead when he frowned. "Let me tell you something about weight loss and your body, Nathaniel. Your body is like a machine, you see. It requires fuel, just like an automobile engine, in order to function and do work. The fuel you give your body is food. Do you understand that?" Nod-nod.

"Yes."

"Good. Now then, when you give your body—your machine—more fuel than it needs to do work, why then it stores that fuel away. Do you know how the body stores that excess fuel?" Shake-shake.

"No."

"It changes the extra fuel you take in to fat, Nathaniel, and holds on to it. That's right . . . fat is extra fuel. Food you have eaten and not used."

This was very interesting to me. Now I understood why I had all those extra pounds on my body. I had either taken in too much fuel, or not done enough work.

"It's all a matter of balance," Dr. Skinny went on. "'Eat just the right amount of food every day and you will neither gain nor lose weight. Eat too much, and you store some food away as fat. Eat *less* than you need, however, and the body will burn up that stored fat . . . and you lose weight. It's simple, really."

"What if I didn't eat anything?" I asked.

Dr. Skinny smiled. "Then your body would burn

54

only the fat you've stored away and you would lose weight very quickly."

That was what I thought. I could probably not eat for a *month* before I burned up all my fat. Somebody as huge as Richard or Hog could probably not eat for a *year* before they lost their fat.

"Not eating at all is unhealthy, though," Dr. Skinny said. "I wouldn't recommend it. Just eat the food we give you, Nathaniel, play hard all day, and you will lose weight." He looked straight into my eyes. "You have been playing hard, haven't you?" Nod-nod.

"Yes, sir. Swimming, baseball, tennis . . ."

"Good. And you have been eating only the food in the dining hall, isn't that right?" Nod-nod.

I thought about the peanuts and candies in Richard's tennis ball cans, and all those bad-tasting cheese sandwiches I'd been stuffing myself with at night. And I lied. "Yes, sir."

"Fine." Dr. Skinny stood up and came around his desk. "Three pounds lost is still three pounds," he said. "Don't lose heart, Nathaniel, because you haven't been losing weight more quickly. There's still five weeks of camp left. I think you'll lose the seventeen pounds you want to and reach your goal." He patted me on the arm. "Work at it, boy," he said. "That's all you have to do, work at it."

"I will, Doctor," I lied again.

When I left Dr. Skinny's office and walked across the grassy square outside, I felt like one of the biggest rats in the history of the world. Here I was with a chance to lose all the weight I wanted to lose (I *think* I wanted to lose) and I was cheating by sneaking extra goodies. Who was I cheating? Why, myself, of course.

I felt so bad about all this, I only had one cheese sandwich that night, not two.

11

The best day and the worst day in camp is Visiting Day. It's the best because your parents come up to see you and you feel so terrific hugging and kissing them, and talking to them all day long. The bad part is when they have to leave, and you know that lonely feeling is going to come back even worse than before.

I hung out with the gang that morning, after breakfast, and we waited out by the road where visitors' cars would come by. There were no activities in camp on Visiting Day, and all the kids were strung out along this dirt path that came off the paved road. Breakfast was over at nine, but the first car didn't come along until almost ten o'clock. It was a long wait. But then the cars started coming along in bunches, and pretty soon there were my parents, and Grandma, waving from the backseat. I ran alongside the car until Dad parked it, and then stuck my head right inside the window and kissed my mom. "Neddie, Neddie," she said, and she wouldn't let go of me. And what's more, I didn't care.

Finally, after about a million hugs and kisses from everybody, especially Grandma, we started walking around the camp and I showed them everything. The swimming pool, the ball fields, the dining hall, and finally my bunk.

They kept telling me how good I looked, how brown and suntanned, and how I looked like I had lost weight. When I told them it was only three pounds so far, they didn't look disappointed. "Great!" my dad said. "Good work, Ned."

I, on the other hand, knew that compared to some of the other kids, I hadn't done well at all.

When we were all coming out of the bunk, Richard came along with his parents. Mr. and Mrs. Napoli were very *big* people, and I'm saying big to be nice. Mr. Napoli was built like a square refrigerator, with a great big belly that hung over his plaid slacks. Mrs. Napoli was wearing a khaki dress and she looked like a tent that could walk. I could see that Richard inherited his weight from them.

"So, you're Ned," Mr. Napoli said after Richard and I had introduced our parents to each other. "Roly says you're his best friend in camp."

"Roly? Who's Roly?"

"Oh, Pop," Richard said, "nobody here calls me that."

Mr. Napoli looked embarrassed. "I guess I spilled the beans," he said. "I'm sorry. Roly is Richard's nickname at home."

"And if you tell anyone up here," Richard said to me, "I'll kill you."

Roly Napoli. It took a few seconds before it sunk in.

"Why don't you folks have lunch with us," Richard's mother said. "I've got tons of stuff." She was carrying a wicker basket about as big as a suitcase.

"She spent all day yesterday cooking," Mr. Napoli smiled.

"That sounds fine," Mom said.

Grandma nudged Mom and gave her a look. "You see," she said. "I could have brought up all Neddie's favorites."

My dad cleared his throat loudly. "Actually, we're supposed to pick up lunchboxes in the dining hall," he said. "So why don't we, Ned."

Dad and I peeled off and headed for the dining hall, leaving Mom and Grandma with the Napolis. Mrs. Napoli was spreading a big blanket on the ground under some trees.

"I told you that parents would bring food up," I said. "But you wouldn't listen."

Dad kind of sighed. "Neddie, there are rules," he said. "Some people live by them, and others don't. I can't understand how you can send kids away to lose weight, and then bring up foods they shouldn't have. It's self-defeating."

"It's only one day," I said. "A kind of treat."

We got into the long line of parents and campers who were filing through the dining hall. "We'll talk about this later," Dad said, which usually meant we

59

wouldn't talk about it at all. When we reached the head of the line, Dad paid some money and we got lunchboxes. They had chicken in them, a little cup of cole slaw, a tomato, two stalks of celery, and an apple.

Richard was up to his nose in food when we got back. He had a paper plate full of salami, peppers, and cheese up to his face and he was shoveling it in as fast as he could.

"He loves my antipasto," Mrs. Napoli said.

"Roly's on a seafood diet," Mr. Napoli said, winking at Richard.

"I see food and I eat it," Richard said. Mr. Napoli laughed and slapped his knee.

"Come, eat," Mrs. Napoli said. She filled a plate for me and I sat down with the others around the blanket.

And that was just the beginning of the feast.

There was Italian bread that somehow was still warm, and smeared with butter that had a little garlic in it. It was delicious. And hot spaghetti with a terrific tomato sauce. And fat sausages I thought would be too spicy but were not. And breaded veal cutlets that were almost as good as the kind Grandma makes. And soda for Richard and me, and wine for all the adults.

I was stuffed and happy for the first time that summer. Richard and I looked at each other and grinned like two idiots.

"Now for dessert," Mrs. Napoli said. She unwrapped a bakery box and when Richard saw it he yelled. "Scotti's! You went to Scotti's Bakery!"

There were all kinds of little cakes in that box that I had never eaten before. Wet ones, that tasted a little

60

like rum, chocolate ones, with a custardy cream inside, and a thin crispy one that had a creamy filling. Cannoli, Mrs. Napoli called the crispy one, and it was great.

When we finished eating, Mr. Napoli lit up a little twisted cigar and burped very loud. "That was a meal and a half," he said. "If I was home now, I'd go take a little nap."

"It was all delicious," my dad said to Mrs. Napoli, "thank you. But after a meal like this, I like to take a stroll." He stood up and looked at me. "Neddie, come on."

We walked across the ball field and I took Dad to the Nature Trail that went through the woods. "Richard seems like a very nice boy," Dad said.

"He's okay."

"Does he like it up here any more than you do?" Dad asked.

"He hates it," I said.

Dad smiled his thin smile. "Does anyone like it?"

"How could anyone like it?" I said. "This place sucks."

Dad stopped walking and looked sternly at me. "Language, Nathaniel," he said. "Watch it."

"Everyone says 'sucks' up here, Dad."

"I am not everyone," Dad said. "I'm your father."

"I'm sorry. This place stinks."

Dad nodded and we started walking again. "Can you put your finger on it, Ned? What . . . *exactly*, is so bad about Camp Lean-Too?"

"You mean besides *everything*?"

Dad laughed and put his arms around me. "Poor Neddie," he said, "you really do hate it up here."

"It's the pits, Dad."

"That bad?"

"Worse," I said.

We walked through a small clearing along the trail, then took the path that led back toward camp. A chipmunk darted across the path in front of us and scampered into the trees. "Listen, Ned," Dad said, "I'm sorry to hear you hate this place so much. But you've got to stick it out, son. Counting from today, there are only twenty-seven more days of camp left. You're more than halfway there."

"It's a long time, Dad. Twenty-seven days . . ."

"Less than half of what you faced when you came up here, though. Think of that, Ned. You got on a bus, you didn't know anyone, and you had two whole months in front of you. It's easier now, you have friends, and you know what to expect."

"I know what to expect all right," I said. "Nothing."

Dad sighed. "Come on, boy, buck up. It's not the end of the world. Think of it as an opportunity. If you lose five pounds a week for the next four weeks, you may not have to diet when you come home. Isn't that worth doing?"

Five pounds a week? Dad had to be kidding. How could I lose five pounds a week when I'd only lost three pounds since I'd been up there? It was impossible. And yet I knew my father and how much he always wanted me to agree with what he said. "Yeah," I said, not believing it for a second, "that would be terrific."

If I lose five pounds a week, I thought, it wouldn't only be terrific, it'd be a miracle.

We walked back across the ball field and already I was beginning to get that end-of-Visiting-Day feeling inside me. It's not a good feeling.

Mrs. Napoli and Mom were talking when we got back. "Richard's always been that way," Mrs. Napoli was saying. "He weighed ten pounds, six ounces when he was born. And he's always been a good eater."

"Not Neddie," Mom said. "In fact, he was so skinny until he was six that we worried about it."

"Richard has big bones," Mrs. Napoli said. "He takes after his father."

Richard looked at me and rolled his eyes in a comical way. He was eating the last cannoli in the cake box.

There was an announcement over the loudspeaker, and for a second I thought they were going to say Visiting Day was over. "Attention, parents . . . we ask you once again not to leave food you may have brought with you. Please do not give campers any food of any kind when you leave here. If you do, it will be confiscated. We thank you for your cooperation."

Dad looked at the remains of Mrs. Napoli's great feast. "I don't think there is anything left to leave," he grinned.

I felt a tugging at my sleeve, and turned to see Grandma behind me. "Come," she said very quietly. I followed her and we walked toward my bunk. We sat down on the steps.

"You look terrible," Grandma said.

"I am terrible."

She gave my head a squeeze. "They're starving you, right?"

"Right."

Grandma shook her head. She looked very angry. "It's wrong," she said. "You're only a little boy and who knows how you'll grow up? I think in a few years you'll shoot up and be a string bean, like Jamie, and you won't be fat anymore. But your parents want you to stay, so you'll stay here. My daughter, bless her heart, can be a real stubborn Susie when she wants to." Grandma sighed one of her "ay-yi-yi" sighs and opened her big handbag. "I got some cookies for you," she said. "And if they weren't inspecting me like a Gestapo I would have brought more." She took a plastic bag of cookies out of her handbag.

"Come inside the bunk," I said. "If anyone sees these cookies, they'll take them away." We went inside and I took the cookies. And gave her one of my best hugs and kisses. I knew how to hide stuff now, thanks to Richard, and I filled my two cans of tennis balls with cookies, and then filled two of Richard's and stuck them in my trunk.

Grandma couldn't believe what I was doing. But she caught on. "So close they watch you?" she asked.

"Yes."

"But you fool them even so, right?"

I grinned at her. Then I told her about Richard's snacks and the raid we had pulled on the kitchen. She didn't like that very much.

"Be careful," she told me, "and don't go stealing. That you shouldn't do. And remember, soon you'll be home and your grandma will take care of you." She opened her handbag and took out a small lace handkerchief and wiped her eyes. I think she might have been crying. "They take a good child and they make him a thief," she said.

A little while after Grandma and I got back to where everyone was sitting, they made the announcement that Visiting Day was over. I walked my parents and Grandma to their car. We said our good-byes, and in spite of trying so hard not to, a few tears came to my eyes. "See you soon, Neddie," my mom said just before the car pulled away. I ran alongside the car while it went slowly, getting one last look at Grandma and my parents while I could. Then the car turned onto the paved road and went away out of sight. All the kids in camp, it looked like, were bunched up by the road, and there wasn't a happy face in sight. About half of them, like me, were crying their heads off.

I rubbed my fists in my eyes until the tears stopped, then I walked back to the bunk.

When I got inside, I gobbled up a whole tennis can full of cookies.

12

It's a good thing I ate so many of Grandma's cookies when I had the chance. Because that very night, they were gone.

Gregg came into the bunk right after supper. "All right, you guys," he said, "everybody open your camp trunks. It's inspection time."

And then Gregg did a very suspicious thing. He went right to Richard's trunk, dug down deep in it, and pulled out all the tennis ball cans he saw. Richard had a funny look on his face, although he had nothing to lose anymore. We had finished all the goodies a week ago. "Why do you have only one tennis ball in each can?" Gregg wanted to know.

"Why not?" Richard shrugged.

"Richard," Gregg said, "I haven't seen you out on the tennis courts once this summer."

"So," said Richard, "that doesn't mean I won't play *some* time."

Gregg shook his head. He smelled the tennis cans. "You had food in here, didn't you?"

"I'll never tell," Richard said. He gave Brian and Fred a nasty look. "Which is more than I can say for some guys in this bunk."

Gregg looked through Hog and Max's stuff next. Naturally, he didn't find anything. And then he went to my trunk. It took him only about a minute to find my stash of cookies. "Oh, Nathaniel," he said, "I'm disappointed."

"I'm sorry," I said. "I got them from my grandma today."

"I'm surprised at her. She knew she wasn't supposed to leave any food with you."

"You don't know my grandma," I said.

"I'll have to take these," Gregg said. He handed me my tennis balls and took the cans. Then he looked through Brian and Fred's trunks. Naturally, he didn't find any food there. "All right," he said, standing in the doorway just before leaving, "I'm putting you guys on notice. From now on, I'm going to be on your trail. Dr. Skinner has looked at all your charts in the office. There are six of you in this bunk, and only two guys have lost the weight they should. I'd say that's highly suspicious, wouldn't you?" Gregg smiled in a funny way, showing all his teeth. "Watch it," he said. Then he left.

We all stared at the door for a few seconds, no one saying anything. Then Max piped up. "We're in trouble."

"How'd they know about Ned's stash?" Richard said. "Did you see the way Gregg went right to the tennis ball cans?" He looked straight at Brian Hume. "Is there a spy in this bunk?"

Brian looked Richard in the eyeballs. "Don't look at me," he said. "I think you guys are nuts, but I don't rat on anybody."

"And neither do I," said Fred Mastric.

"If you guys want to waste your whole summer, go ahead," Brian said. "But if you just forget about stealing extra snacks, you can have fun up here. And you'll lose weight, too."

"That's right," Fred said. "You can even reach your target weight."

Richard smiled. "You want to know what my target is? A pizza, loaded with drippy cheese and sauce."

"Don't say that," Max said, licking his lips. "It makes me too hungry."

"My target is a hot fudge sundae," Hog said. He had a kind of dreamy look in his eyes. "Picture it. Vanilla ice cream, two scoops, and the hot fudge is dripping all over it . . . with lots of nuts and whipped cream, and a cherry on top . . ."

"Oh, God," Max whined, "cut it out, I'm dying . . ." He threw his arms out and fell to the floor, making believe he was dying. "Save me, somebody," he croaked. "Bring me a big slice of my mom's peach pie . . . with vanilla ice cream on top."

Hog knelt down beside Max. He took his pulse like a doctor. "I'm sorry, son," he said, "but we're all out of peach pie. I'm afraid you're going to die."

Richard and I were cracking up, and even Brian was smiling.

"Then give me *chocolate* ice cream and my mother's peach pie," Max said.

"Son, we don't have any of your mother's peach pie."

"I don't care," Max said, "give me *strawberry* ice cream and my mom's peach pie."

"Look, son," Hog said, "you may be dying but I've got to tell you this. *We don't have your mother's peach pie!*"

"All right, then," Max said, "forget the ice cream. I'll just have a piece of my mother's peach pie . . ."

13

We were playing tennis. At least, that's what we were supposed to be doing. Richard and me against Max Cohen and Hog. But it was very hot, and nobody seemed to be too athletic. Richard just wanted to stand at the net and smash every ball that came to him. And I mean came right to him, because he wouldn't move one step either way to hit a ball. So I was running all around the backcourt chasing down almost everything.

We took a break and sat down in the shade, under a big pine tree. "We've got to get into town," Richard said.

"What's so important about getting into town?" Max asked.

"Because that's where the food is, dummy," Richard said. "Do you enjoy starving to death?"

Between Gregg watching us so closely and the end of our private supply of goodies, we had eaten nothing but camp food for five days.

70

"I don't think we'll make it into town," I said.

"I'm not giving up," Richard said. He looked at Hog, who seemed to know what Richard was thinking.

"Oh, no," Hog said, "I'm not fiddling with my braces again."

Richard put an innocent look on his face. "Did I say anything?"

"You were going to," Hog said. "Last year he talked me into it. I picked at my braces until I got a wire loose, then they had to send me into town to see the orthodontist."

"It worked, didn't it?" Richard said.

"Yeah, it worked," said Hog. "Everybody chipped in and I bought a ton of candy bars. But I'm not going to do it again."

"Why not?"

"Because it's my mouth, that's why, and that stupid orthodontist hurt last time."

"Okay, okay," Richard said.

We sat around thinking for a while, staring up at the big puffy white clouds drifting by.

"Hog," Richard said, "we could break your eyeglasses."

"Uh-uh," Hog said. "No way. Without my glasses I can't see a thing."

"Come on," Richard said.

"No," said Hog. He sounded like he meant it.

"I got an idea," Max said. "You see this sneaker?" He showed us the side of his tennis sneaker, which had the beginning of a crack in it. "What if I ripped it the rest of the way so I couldn't wear it anymore? They'd have to send me into town to buy a new pair, wouldn't they?"

"Maybe yes and maybe no," Hog said.

"It's worth a try," Richard said.

"Good-bye, sneaker," Max said. He took it off his foot and began working at the small crack, which turned into a big hole in about two minutes. "How does that look?" he asked.

"Like a torn sneaker," I said.

"We'll have to pool our money," Richard said. "I've got twenty-five dollars."

I had ten dollars of my own, squirreled away in the bottom of my toothbrush holder. Max had twenty and Hog thirty. By the end of the day the plan was set. Max was to go into town after breakfast. He would take fifty dollars and a shopping list with him. The first stop was the shoe store, the second one was the super-market.

We watched Max go off in the camp pickup truck the next morning. One of the older staff, Gertie, the nurse, went with him.

Max showed up at the bunk just before lunch. Empty-handed. "I didn't have a chance," he said. "I just bought new sneakers and got back into the truck. Gertie didn't leave me alone for a second." He handed us back our money. I went into the bathroom to put my ten dollars back into my toothbrush holder. Richard came in and went to the urinal. "Somewhere in this camp," he said, unzipping his fly, "there has to be someone who wants to make a dishonest dollar."

14

"One hundred and ten pounds," Dr. Skinny exclaimed as I stepped off the scale. "That's really excellent, Nathaniel. You are doing well, aren't you?" Nod-nod.

"Looks that way." Sure I was doing well. I was also walking around so hungry I could eat a tree.

"It takes some children longer than others to begin losing weight. But, sooner or later, all of our campers get into a healthy weight-loss pattern."

Sure they do. When their secret supply of goodies runs out and they only have that rotten Camp Lean-Too food to eat.

"You've lost eight pounds so far, Nathaniel. Twelve pounds more and you'll reach your target weight. I'm sure you'll like going home weighing twenty pounds less than when you came here." Nod-nod.

"Yeah. That'll be terrific."

"Your parents will be pleased, won't they?" Nod-nod.

"Uh-huh."

Dr. Skinny stepped back and measured me with his eyes. "I even think those eight pounds are beginning to show," he said. He put a finger inside the waistband of my jeans and tugged. "They feel a little loose to me."

I could hardly believe it, but for once Dr. Skinny was correct. The jeans I was wearing always pinched me around the waist, but now that I thought about it, they didn't feel that way today.

"One more thing," Dr. Skinny said. "Gregory reported finding cookies in your trunk just after Visiting Day. I'm sure they must have looked very tempting to you." Nod-nod.

"They were better than tempting. They were delicious."

"I'm sure. But, Nathaniel, you must remember . . . snacking is your enemy. You really don't want to spoil your progress by eating cookies and candy, do you?" Shake-shake.

"Oh, no, sir!"

"Splendid!" said Dr. Skinny, smiling. "Keep up the good work and see you next week."

Sure I'd see him next week . . . if I didn't perish from hunger in the meantime.

In school one time, we learned about this old Greek guy who walked around all day carrying a lantern, looking for an honest man. Richard was just the opposite of him. He was walking around Camp Lean-Too, searching for a *dis*honest man.

74

And he found him.

"His name is Lem," Richard announced one day, "one of the high school kids from town who cut the grass. Lem said he'd take me into town one afternoon when he finishes work."

It was resting time, after lunch, and I was sitting in the shady spot behind our bunk. Max and Hog were inside, writing letters.

"That's great," I said, without much enthusiasm. I was feeling kind of low. I had a lot of things on my mind. "You know you're not allowed to leave camp without permission."

"A detail," Richard said.

"You could get into trouble," I said.

"What'll they do?" Richard grinned. "Send me home?"

Richard looked so bubbly and happy it cheered me up a little. "How come this guy Lem is willing to take you?" I asked. "He could get into trouble, too, if they found out about it."

Richard looked at me like I was the class idiot. "For money, that's why. Fifteen bucks, round trip."

"Wow! That's a lot of money, Rich."

"He wanted twenty," Richard said. "I had to bargain like crazy."

"Fifteen bucks . . ."

"Yeah," Richard said, "it's highway robbery. But remember, there's seven miles of highway into town and seven miles back."

"But what if you get caught?" I asked.

"Don't worry about it, I won't," Richard said. He gave me a funny look. "Are you all right, Ned?"

"I don't know."

"You feel sick?"

"Not exactly . . ."

"Uh-oh," Richard said, "it's that last-weeks-of-camp weirdness." He sat down next to me and leaned against the wall of the bunk. "They're getting to you, aren't they? Dr. Skinny and all his crap."

"Maybe," I said. "It seems to me we spend all our time scheming and planning to get goodies. Maybe we ought to just forget about it."

"Have you been talking to Brian Goodboy?" Richard sneered. That was his name for Brian Hume.

"It's not that," I said.

"What then?"

"I told you, I don't know . . ."

"It's the old conscience, huh?" Richard said. "You're going to put on a big weight-losing drive until the end of camp so you can go home and make your folks proud of you, right?"

"Maybe," I said.

Richard grabbed my arm. "That's sucker stuff, Ned!" His brown eyes were wide and the look on his face was fierce. "Who made you fat in the first place, dummy? Your parents, that's who. You don't feed yourself. All that food they rammed down your throat, everything they taught you to like. They're the ones who fattened you up and now they don't like it. So instead of helping you at home they send you away to a

76

stinking place like this to do their dirty work for them. Don't you understand that?"

The way Richard looked, I didn't want to argue.

"My great-grandfather came from Rome," Richard said. "You know about the Romans? They practically invented eating. They'd sit down and stuff themselves until they couldn't eat anymore and then they'd go to this room—they called it a vomitorium—and they'd make themselves throw up by putting a finger down their throats. And then when their stomachs were empty, they'd go back and eat some more. That's the God's honest truth, Ned."

"That's weird," I said.

"You want to talk weird, look at my parents. You saw them, didn't you? When do *they* go on a diet, huh? They eat like food is going to disappear tomorrow. I get pasta at home five nights a week. And pies and cakes and cookies and every damn thing I want. And then they look at me in spring and it's 'You're getting too fat, Roly. Gotta send you to Camp Lean-Too again, Roly!' You get it, Ned? They're the ones with the problem, and I get sent up here."

"It's not right."

"Damn straight it's not right."

"But it's not that way in my house, Rich."

"You don't do the cooking, do you?"

"No. But . . ."

"Then it's the same thing, kiddo."

"But my parents don't eat that way. It's not the same thing."

"Somebody's been feeding you pretty good, Ned. Who was it, the Tooth Fairy?"

An answer came to the tip of my tongue, but I swallowed it back again. I knew who was feeding me, all right. But it was very hard to think about, and impossible to say.

"Somebody taught you to eat the way you do, and it wasn't you," Richard said. "That's why, when I get a chance to get my hands on something good to eat, I'm gonna take it. Now are you with me, or not?"

"I'm not going into town," I said.

"Of course not, dummy, *I'm* going. But will you help me?"

"Sure."

Richard grinned and punched my arm. "Now we're getting someplace," he said.

15

I used to think that people who were criminals were all ugly and horrible looking. But there was Lem Samuels, the kid who was going to smuggle Richard up and back to Hartleyville for money, and he looked very ordinary. Blond hair, brown eyes, a couple of pimples on his chin. Lem looked like your ordinary high school kid who was old enough to drive a car. And his beat-up Chevy looked pretty ordinary, too. It was dirty and dusty, and the right rear fender was bashed in.

Getting Richard out of camp and into town with Lem turned out to be easy. Richard sneaked away from our group as we were walking to the big ball field to play softball. One second he was right behind me and then—*zoom*—he just made a sharp right turn and disappeared into the trees. It was about four in the afternoon, when Lem would be leaving to go home.

Hog, Max, and myself were all set to make excuses for Richard not being at the ball game, but no one even asked!

About five thirty, when we were back at the bunk and waiting to go to dinner, Richard came walking in. He winked at me and put his finger to his lips.

"Did you get the stuff?" Max asked, and Richard shot him a dirty look. "Oolitcay," Richard whispered, glancing over at Brian and Fred. He walked outside and we followed.

"We're all set," Richard said when we were away from the bunk. "And Max, keep your mouth shut in front of Brian. I don't trust him."

"What'd you get?" Hog asked.

"Everything," Richard said.

"Ooh! Ooh!" Hog squealed. Behind his glasses, his eyes were lighting up. "Where is it? I want some!"

"Nobody gets nothing till after supper," Richard said.

"Did you get Hershey bars?" Max asked.

Richard nodded. "I got everything we said to get."

"Oh, God!" Max said. "Unlimited candy bars!"

"Will you guys relax!" Richard ordered. "Now calm down and stop acting like babies. I'm the guy who took the chance and I'm in charge of the stash. And this time, nobody is going to take it away. But we've got to be very careful and act normal."

"Can't we skip supper?" Hog said.

Richard scowled. "That's just what I mean, dummy. We've got Gregg and everyone else right on our tails. Now cool it."

Supper turned out to be a very interesting meal. Because for once, we all knew that it was going to be followed by a real dessert. Naturally, we didn't eat very much.

After supper, in our free time period, we took a walk to the big ball field. Just beyond it, and next to the gravel car park, was a rusty shed. They kept tools in there, and the lawn mowers. We turned the corner and walked inside the shed.

Richard went to the back, where there was a kind of bin. He pulled away a bunch of dirty rags and there it was! A couple of big shopping bags, loaded with goodies. Candy bars in six-packs! Corn chips! Pretzels!

Hog squealed and Max was groaning. "Take it easy," Richard said. "Now, we're only going to take a few things and go into the woods. No eating in here."

"You bought enough to last about a year," I said.

"You know it," Richard grinned. "The checkout girl asked me if I was buying stuff for a party. I told her, yes, it's for a party all right."

Hog took a half-pound package of M&M's and a six-pack of Almond Joys. Max took two packs of Hershey bars. He loved Hershey bars. I took a pack of Milky Ways and Richard took a pack of Nestlé's Crunch and a bag of pretzels. Before we went into the woods, Richard was very careful about covering up the stash with the dirty rags.

And back in the woods we had our party.

Max was lying back on the ground, hugging himself and moaning. "I must have died and gone to heaven," he was saying.

Hog's big cheeks were puffed up with candy, but he managed to grin just the same. "Take that, Camp Lean-Too," he said between mouthfuls.

Richard attacked his candy bars like they were the enemy. One after another he shoved them inside his mouth, taking time out only to throw a couple of pretzels in, too.

I have to tell you, in spite of all the candy we ate, the eating of it didn't take very long. When we were finished, we were all lying on our backs, looking up at the sky through the trees. I think we were overcome with happiness, because no one spoke for a long time. Finally, Max piped up. "Can I get some more?" he asked Richard.

"No," Richard said.

"Please?"

"Control yourself," Richard said. "We'll do it again tomorrow night."

"Can't I take back something for a snack before bed?" Hog asked.

Richard sat up. "No, dummy," he said. "We only eat our stuff out here, where no one can see, and we only do it after supper."

"What if I want some after lunch?" Hog said. "It's my candy, Rich. I paid for it."

"Look, you guys," Richard said, "I'm the boss of this stash and don't forget it." He gave Hog a hard look. "Pick up all the wrappers, Hog. And take them back in the woods and hide them good."

Hog stared at Richard for a second, then looked at me. He didn't say anything.

82

"Move it, Hog," Richard ordered.

"Who made you my boss?" Hog said. I could tell by the way he said it that Hog didn't mean it. His voice was shaky.

Richard stood up and looked down at Hog. Then he kicked him in the butt, not too hard. "Move it!" he said.

"Come on, Rich," I said. "Don't start a fight."

Richard wheeled around and glared at me. "I stick my neck out for you guys and this is what I get, huh? I thought you were my friend, Ned."

"I am your friend, Rich."

"Then who's the boss here?"

Max was staring at the ground, shaking his head a little from side to side. He hated this whole scene as much as me.

"You're the boss, okay?" I said. "Now do you feel better?"

Richard kind of snorted with his nose. Hog began picking up the candy wrappers. Richard sat down next to me. He gave me a friendly slap on the arm. "Now then," he said, "on the way back to camp with Lem we got a great idea. I don't know who thought of it first, me or Lem, but he was laughing about how desperate we are for candy and goodies. And I said that probably all the kids in Camp Lean-Too would pay anything to get their hands on what I was bringing back to camp. That's true, isn't it?"

"Probably," I said.

"There you are," he said. "That's the idea. I'll bet we make a pile of money."

"Wait a minute," I said, *what's* the idea?"

"We're all gonna be partners," Richard said. "We're gonna sell candy bars to the other campers for a dollar apiece!"

16

For the first time that summer, I was having a hard time sleeping. A lot of feelings and ideas kept racing through my mind. Up above me the bedsprings groaned every time Hog turned in his sleep. A patch of moonlight was shining through the window and I could see the outline of Richard's face buried in his pillow.

Something was bothering me.

Deep down in my heart, or my mind or soul or wherever you feel things, I knew that going out and selling candy bars to all the other campers wasn't right. It was just plain wrong.

But exactly *why* I knew it was wrong was hard to figure out.

What was the difference, I wondered, between the four of us sneaking candy into camp and offering the same goodies to everybody else?

If we could have a great time, why shouldn't we let all the other kids in on it? Was that wrong?

I thought about Brian Hume and Fred Mastric, sleeping just two beds away toward the corner of the bunk. They hadn't had any treats since the first day in camp. And every time our gang had goodies, even those awful cheese sandwiches, they didn't want any. Brian had lost sixteen pounds so far, and Fred had lost twenty. Fred could stick his hand inside the waist of his jeans and pull it way away from his stomach. He and Brian were very proud of how much weight they had lost. Would it be fair for us to ruin all their hard work in losing weight by tempting them with candy bars?

No way, I thought to myself. It was wrong, wrong, wrong.

It was a strange thing about Richard. I liked him so much, and yet there were things about him I didn't like. Wanting to be the boss of our gang, for instance. And kicking Hog to *prove* he was. Richard had always been the leader. Why did he have to go prove it like that?

Richard was funny and nice and easy to talk to and helpful and an interesting person to be with. But there was this other side of him I didn't understand at all. And didn't like.

That was what was mixing me up, and why I couldn't sleep.

Tomorrow Richard was going to want me to help him start selling candy bars. And I just wasn't going to do it.

So what would happen? Richard would be mad, that

was for sure. What would he do when I said no? Would he kick me in the butt, like Hog? Beat me up? Stop talking to me? Would he get the other guys to stop talking to me, too, and make me an outcast?

He would probably do all those things, I figured. And I, being the chicken kid of all times, would probably not do a thing about it.

Breakfast was probably the closest thing to a regular meal at Camp Lean-Too. We got poached eggs twice a week, which they served on some kind of tan toasted bread. It wasn't too bad. The rest of the week we got cold cereal and skim milk. And with no sugar anywhere in sight, it wasn't too good. But this was a poached egg morning, with an orange to carry away for dessert.

We played basketball the first period. At least, that's what we were supposed to be playing. Max had a hard time dribbling. The whole summer he had not learned that you can't dribble a ball off your own foot. That's why nobody ever passed him the ball. And Hog was not much of a basketball player, either. The first time I saw him shoot a jump shot I almost cracked up. He kind of took the ball, put his arms over his head, then jumped. Of course, he only lifted about a half-inch off the ground. It was the lowest jump shot in history.

Richard favored the hook shot. All he wanted to do was stand at the foul line and call for the ball, his back toward the basket. Then, when he got it, he'd sort of wheel around on one foot and curl his back arm, and then fling up a crazy shot while looking at the basket over his shoulder. He didn't make very many.

It wasn't until we were on our way to arts and crafts that Richard brought up selling the candy bars. "After lunch," he said, "we'll talk about you-know-what." He winked at me and grinned. "I think I've got it all figured out."

In arts and crafts I was finishing up these nameplates for my family. They were made out of small pieces of wood which I had sanded and lacquered. The letters on them were all alphabet macaroni. I had made a Mom, Dad, and Grandma nameplate already, and now I was finishing one for Jamie and another for Elizabeth. I was having trouble fitting in all the letters on the one for Elizabeth, which is just as long a name as Nathaniel. I had to crowd the "t" and the "h" together at the end, but it looked all right. Although there are a lot of things I'm good at, arts and crafts is not one of them.

Finally, lunch was over and we were sitting in the shade behind the bunk. Richard was explaining how we would begin selling candy bars. His idea was that Max, Hog, and me would circulate around the camp. We were supposed to walk up to campers, one at a time, and say something like: "Hey kid, want to buy a candy bar?"

If they did, we would tell them to go to the clump of trees at the end of the big ball field. Richard was going to take it from there, making sure nobody saw where the stash was hidden.

89

I sat there, listening to Richard giving orders, and I knew in my heart I wasn't going to do any of it. To tell you the truth, I was scared.

"Start this afternoon," Richard was saying, "but nobody gets any candy until supper break. Okay, you guys?"

"Richard," I heard myself saying, "I'm not going to do it."

He looked at me, then at Hog and Max, and then back to me. "Not going to do what?"

I cleared my throat. "I'm not going to sell any candy, Rich. I think it's a bad idea, and wrong, too."

"Are you nuts?" Richard said. "We'll make a fortune!"

"I don't care about that," I said.

"What are you . . . scared?"

"Yes," I said.

"I'm scared, too," Max said. "We'll get caught for sure."

"Shut up!" Richard yelled at Max. "I'm talking to Ned."

Hearing Max speak up made me feel better. And then Richard stood up over me and that made me feel scared again. "Am I the boss of the stash or not?"

"You're the boss," I said.

"Damn right!"

"But I'm not going to do it," I said.

"Oh, yes, you are," Richard said.

"Oh, no, I'm not," I said, and then Richard leaned down and yanked me by my shirt so I stood up next to him.

"Why not?" Richard said.

"It's wrong," I said. "It's unfair to all the other kids who really want to diet."

Richard kind of threw his eyeballs up to the sky. "Jesus," he said, "you're a moron."

"I'm sorry," I said.

"Don't you want to make money?"

"Not particularly."

"Don't you want to have a big fat laugh on the stupid people who run this stupid camp?"

I shrugged. I'd never even thought about that idea.

"Put up your fists," Richard said as he put his up.

I kept my hands at my sides.

"Come on," Richard said. "I'm going to whip your butt," except he didn't say butt.

I shook my head. "No."

Richard punched me in the shoulder. It hurt.

"What are you, too yellow to fight?" Richard said.

I didn't answer, mostly because I was afraid I'd start blubbering if I opened my mouth.

Richard grabbed me by the arm and started pulling me into the woods. I tried to shake him off but his grip was too tight, and I ended up with my arm bent behind my back. He pushed me into a clearing, where no one could see us from the bunk.

"Come on," Richard said. "Start swinging." He kind of stuck out his face near me so I could hit him.

"I don't want to fight," I said.

"Why not?"

"Because you'll kill me."

91

"I'll kill you anyway," Richard said. He pushed my shoulder. I didn't do anything. "Come on," he said.

"No."

He looked at me for a second, kind of staring. "You're so chicken it's impossible," he said. "Didn't you ever fight anyone before?"

I shook my head.

"Never?"

"No," I said.

"You have to fight sometimes," he said. "What if someone was picking on you? You'd fight then, wouldn't you?"

"I don't know."

"What if he called your mother a dirty name? Would you let him get away with that?"

"Probably. If he was a big kid."

Richard sighed and sat down on a tree stump. "You really are weird, Ned."

"I know I am," I said. "I've always been too scared to fight."

I told Richard about Phil Steinkraus and how he made me and Steve stop taking the bus to school, and how he always calls me Jelly Belly.

"You got to fight him, Ned," Richard said.

I explained how big Phil Steinkraus is and how he'd probably kill me.

"Look at it this way," Richard said. "Which hurts more? Being called Jelly Belly, or maybe getting punched out once or twice?"

I said I really didn't think either was a good idea.

"Sooner or later, you've got to fight back," Richard said.

"Okay," I said, "let it be later."

Richard thought that was funny, and we both laughed. "Are we still friends?" he asked.

I nodded. "I don't know what I would have done in this stupid place except for you," I said. Which was the truth.

"You're my best friend up here," Richard said.

He stuck out his hand and I shook it.

"We won't go around selling candy," I said.

"Nah," said Richard. "It was Lem's idea, and it's stupid."

"What'll we tell Hog and Max then?" I asked. "The last they knew, you were pushing me out here to whip my butt."

Richard thought for a few seconds. "I'm gonna tell them you whipped my butt instead."

17

On the last night of the summer in my old camp they always had a banquet. It was super. All the campers would dress up in the one nice outfit they brought up to camp. There would be special decorations in the dining hall, music, and all the sports and achievement awards were given out. And the food was always the best of the summer, because they served just about everything. There was roast beef *and* chicken, french fries, and a great big cake with second and third portions for all. It was a great night, always, and the next morning on the way home I sometimes felt sad because the summer was over.

Let me tell you about the last-night banquet we had at Camp Lean-Too.

Everybody dressed up for it, but a lot of the kids looked funny. Some of them had lost so much weight that their clothes drooped. Boys had these pants all bunchy in the waist where they had tightened their belts, and one girl was wearing a dress held together with safety pins.

They gave awards, like at Camp Sha-Ka-Nah-Kee, but not for sports. The awards they gave were for Consistent Weight Loss, Best Change in Eating Habits, Most Cooperative Camper, and Best Personal Hygiene. It was sickening.

You'll notice I haven't mentioned the food. Maybe I shouldn't. I mean, if you are not feeling too good you might get sick. This was supposed to be a banquet, a big splurge, a celebration for God's sake! So we all drank a toast with warm tomato juice. Yuch! Then we had a kind of cookout, with hot dogs and hamburgers cooked over a charcoal fire, which sounds great. Except that there wasn't a hot dog roll or a hamburger bun in sight.

Have you ever looked at a naked hot dog burned all black? You want to feed it to your dog, not eat it yourself.

Instead of potato chips or french fries, we had something called crispy carrots. I don't think even Bugs Bunny would like them. And then we got to the dessert, which was supposed to be a cake. It was called Camp Lean-Too Meringue Cake, and it was a big wide cake with a bumpy top. Camp Lean-Too was written on it in green script. All the campers got one measly slice each. It was hard and crunchy and it had soy bean nuts inside, and the best part about it was that it made the skim milk taste better.

After dinner there were awards ceremonies. Dr.

Skinny got up and made a speech. He said we all had a marvelous summer, nod-nod, and we all made good progress, nod-nod, and we won't forget all the good eating habits we learned up here, shake-shake, and things like that. Then Dr. Skinny began calling the names of all the campers one by one, and we each had to walk up to the platform and get a certificate. It was alphabetical, and Max Cohen came back to where we were sitting and we all looked at his certificate. It was a "LEAN-TOO LOSER'S CERTIFICATE" and on it was Max's name and the amount of weight he had lost, which was eleven pounds. Hog came back with his certificate next. He had lost eight pounds, and Dr. Skinny gave Hog a funny look along with the certificate. Maybe because Hog was one of the kids in camp who had lost the least. Richard's certificate said he had lost ten pounds. "One week of my mother's cooking and I'll gain it right back," he said.

They called my name and I walked up to the platform. "Fourteen pounds lost, Nathaniel," Dr. Skinny said as he handed me my certificate. He shook my hand. "Imagine how much you might have lost if you had tried," Dr. Skinny said to me. "See you next year."

One of the counselors near the platform blew a fanfare on his trumpet, and Dr. Skinny put up his arms for silence. "And now," he said, "the last award and the best one we make at Camp Lean-Too. This is the Grand Loser's Award, given to the camper who has lost the most weight this summer." One of the counselors started a drumroll by banging on the top of a garbage can with two sticks. "And the winner . . . with

a certified weight loss of forty-four pounds . . . is . . ."
And Dr. Skinny read off the kid's name, which I didn't
recognize. Everybody began to applaud, and this older
kid from one of the senior bunks came walking to the
platform.

"Forty-four pounds," Hog said. "My kid sister
weighs forty-four pounds. That guy lost as much
weight as a whole, entire person!"

We all looked at the kid who jumped up on the
platform. He was tall and blond, and he looked terrific. I have to tell you, I felt funny as we all applauded him. He looked like a normal guy, not freaky
fat like all of us in our gang. He wouldn't be back at
Camp Lean-Too next year, that was for sure. In fact,
the kid looked so great he probably wouldn't even
have to diet anymore.

Dr. Skinny handed over this gold cup and the kid
held it over his head with two hands, like he'd just
won the Super Bowl or something. Looking at him
smiling up there, something turned over in my gut. I
could have been standing there, I thought, if I hadn't
been nibbling cheese sandwiches and gobbling down
candy bars all summer. I could have been a normal
person by now, with no more dieting, maybe, and no
fat belly and no huge butt. Forty-four pounds lost. If I
had lost forty-four pounds I would weigh seventy-four
pounds now, which is one pound less than I should
weigh. I couldn't imagine myself weighing that little. I
mean, it was hard to get a picture of myself looking
like that kid on the platform.

Max Cohen whispered in my ear. "Let's go have our

own celebration." He said the same thing to Hog and Richard and we began drifting away from the crowd. We cut toward our bunk, then circled around and headed toward the big ball field. Somewhere thunder rumbled, and a far-off flash of lightning lit the sky. Nobody said much as we crossed the field to the shed. I think we all felt a little down.

We went into the shed and Richard shined his flashlight on the stash. "We might as well take it all," Max said. "It's our last night."

"Might as well," Richard said.

We took the shopping bags out of the shed and walked with them into the woods. We settled down in the little clearing we had used so many times before.

"And now," Max said, in a pretty good imitation of Dr. Skinny's voice, "it is time for our annual awards." Max stuck his hand in one of the shopping bags and grabbed a handful of candy bars. "The first award," he said, "is what we at Camp Lean-Too call our 'I'll Eat Anything That Doesn't Eat Me First Award.' It goes to that outstanding camper, Darryl 'Hog' Hawkins."

Richard and I applauded and Max flipped a Hershey bar to Hog. "Thank you, thank you," Hog said, and he bit into the Hershey bar without taking the paper off it.

"You're supposed to unwrap it, dummy," Richard said, and Hog said "Really?" in a funny way that made us all crack up.

"And now," Max pronounced, "we give the Nasty Nosher Award!"

"What a nosher?" Hog asked.

"It means a nibbler," I said.

"Nasty Nosher of the Year, Richard Napoli!" Max said. He gave Richard a bag of M&M's. Richard ripped open the bag and shoved the candy in his mouth until his cheeks puffed out.

"Good work," Max said. "And the last award, for eating above and beyond the call of duty . . . the annual Monster Mouth Award . . . to your friend and mine, Nathaniel 'Neddie' Robbins!" Max tossed me a Chunky bar and I put the whole thing in my mouth. Unlike Hog, I unwrapped it first.

"Speech!" Hog cried. "Speech!"

"Yeah," Richard joined in. "A few words, Monster Mouth."

Did you ever try to talk with a whole candy bar in your mouth? It took a while to get started.

"Friends, Romans, countrymen, and fellow fatties," I began. I knew Richard would like the Romans part. "We are gathered here to celebrate the end of summer. Tomorrow we leave Camp Lean-Too . . ."

"Hooray!" Hog and Max yelled.

". . . and return to our families and home. In a short time, we will be back at school."

"Boo!" Hog said. "Don't say that word."

"As we say good-bye to this lovely place, I ask you . . . what are the lessons we have learned during our summer at Camp Lean-Too?"

"Starvation is no fun," said Hog.

"Right," I said.

"Camp Lean-Too sucks," said Richard.

"Correct," I said. "What else?"

"If you see something good to eat, grab it," said Max, "because you might not get another chance."

Lightning flashed, and thunder crashed very loud, nearby. A breeze came through the woods.

"Very good," I said. "You are all terrific campers. But what is the number one lesson we learned here? Campers?"

"Doctor Skinny is a moron," Hog said.

"No," I said, "that's not it."

"Next time, find a foolproof way of bringing up a stash," Max said.

"Wrong," I said.

"Next time," said Richard, "we find a guy like Lem the *first* week we're up here."

"Uh-uh," I said. "Campers, the number one lesson we should have learned at lovely Camp Lean-Too is this . . . *next time, there shouldn't be any next time!* Because you've got to be crazy to come here more than once."

The wind blew hard and a few drops of rain spattered down on us through the trees. Then, as quickly as that, it started to pour. We all jumped up and started running. "Hey, the stash!" Hog yelled.

"Leave it!" Richard yelled.

"We don't need it," Max hollered. "We're going home!"

We came to the edge of the big ball field and the rain was coming down in barrels and buckets. All of us were soaked through to the skin before we were half-way across the field.

"Home!" yelled Hog.

"Home!" screamed Max.

"Home!" Richard yelled, slipping and sliding.

I yelled it, too, and again, because this was the happiest feeling of the whole summer. Running, slipping, falling and getting up, running across the field in the dark with the rain pouring down, soaking wet and yelling, all of us, running, running, running toward home.

18

"Will you take a look at this boy!" Grandma said before she grabbed me. Then she was squeezing me tight, holding me against her. She smelled like flowers. "How much weight did you lose?" she asked when she let me go.

"Fourteen pounds."

"Ay-yi-yi," she smiled. "He looks like an angel."

"He looks like Neddie to me," Jamie said with a grin. He started to shake my hand and then he grabbed me, too.

"Don't smother the boy," Dad said, "let's go inside." He carried my duffel bag inside the house and set it down in the front hallway.

The house looked funny to me, after being away from it all summer. Smaller, somehow, and not quite the way it had looked before I'd left. Everything was in its right place, but I was a little surprised to see all the things I remembered.

"Are you hungry?" Grandma asked.

"Not really."

"Not even a little?" she said.

"Rose, please," my dad said to Grandma, "he just got home."

"Fresh doughnuts I made," she said. "Would you like one with a glass of milk, maybe?"

She didn't have to tell me about the doughnuts. I could smell them even out there in the front hallway. "Maybe after dinner," I said. "They gave me a box lunch on the bus."

Grandma just nodded, but I could tell she was a little surprised. I hardly ever remember turning down one of her doughnuts before.

Jamie grabbed my duffel bag and took it up to my room. I followed him up the stairs, carrying my travel bag. My room looked like the best place in the world to me. There was my Cardinal pennant, hanging over the bed, and my picture of Ted Simmons on the dresser. The airplane Jamie had made for me when I'd had the mumps two years ago was hanging from the light fixture, slowly swinging. I went across to my desk and looked at my baseball standings board. It had been Jamie's present to me on my last birthday, and it's really neat. It has these little metal discs with all the team insignias, and the board is magnetized so they stick when you put them in place. The standings of the teams were all in the right places.

"You kept my standings board up to date all summer," I said to Jamie.

"Yes."

"Thanks, Jamie."

He sat down on my rocking chair. "Well, I didn't actually," he said. "I just fixed it up this morning, from the standings in the newspaper."

"Well, thanks anyway."

I sat down on my bed and looked at Jamie, rocking slowly in my chair. He smiled at me. "When's Mom coming home?" I asked.

"The usual time," Jamie said. "This is her busy season, or she would have taken the day off to meet you at the bus."

I opened my travel bag and found the nameplates I'd made. I unwrapped Jamie's and gave it to him.

"Thanks," he said, "it's nice. Maybe I'll paste it on the door to my room."

"I made one for everybody."

"Good," Jamie said. He rocked up and back for a few moments. "So," he asked, "what kind of a summer did you have?"

"Terrible."

"Right," said Jamie. "That's just about what you figured you'd have."

"Only it was worse," I said.

Jamie nodded. "You lost fourteen pounds, though. That's okay."

"I was supposed to lose twenty," I said. "And I should have."

Jamie chuckled under his breath. "Let's not talk about 'should haves,'" he said. "I should have been running three-mile training sessions by now, instead of what I've been running."

"What are you running?"

"Oh, quarter-mile sprints . . . half miles, sometimes."

"How's your time?"

"You would ask that," Jamie grinned. "Lousy," he added, "plain lousy."

"So you didn't have a great summer either," I said.

"Oh, I don't know," Jamie said. "I've been working four days a week for Rocco DeVito, mowing lawns. And I've been swimming a lot. It hasn't been too bad."

"There was one kid in camp who lost forty-four pounds," I said.

Jamie whistled through his teeth. "Forty-four pounds, wow!"

"I should have lost more," I said. "And I could have."

Jamie sat way back in the rocker and stretched his long legs out straight. "Well, why didn't you?"

I looked at him looking at me and I knew I had to tell Jamie everything. "Swear you won't tell Mom and Dad?" I said.

Jamie swore and then I told him about Richard and Hog and Max, and the tennis ball cans, and the great raid on the kitchen where we only got these terrible cheese sandwiches. Jamie was laughing a lot. I told him about Lem, and the stash, and how we had these candy bar banquets almost every night. And Jamie laughed some more. "It's a wonder you didn't *gain* weight up there," he said.

"Now you see why I should have lost more?"

"Yes," Jamie said. "You can resist everything except temptation."

"Right."

Jamie stood up to leave. He ruffled up the hair on my head. "You better get ready for temptation," he said, "because Grandma's been cooking her head off all day. It's going to be one great dinner, squirt."

"Oh, God," I said, "here we go again."

19

Well, of course, my mom made a big fuss over me when she came home, and I didn't mind it a bit. She thought I was starting to look thinner. She made me stand off and turn around a few times. "Definitely thinner," she said. "I can see it, Neddie. You're starting to make progress."

I could smell terrific things cooking in the kitchen. And when we all sat down to dinner, there they were on the table.

"Roast chicken," Grandma said as she put a big piece on my plate. "Your favorite." She piled on mashed potatoes and they were another one of my favorites. Grandma makes these fried bits of onion that she mashes into the potato, and I could eat a whole bowl of them.

"Enough," my mom said as Grandma piled potatoes on my plate.

Grandma gave Mom a look and put the plate down

in front of me. "And there's more where that came from," she said.

Dad sighed and kind of shook his head. He didn't say anything, but I could see he was annoyed.

I was back in heaven again. This was chicken that tasted like chicken. I ate very quickly, because everything was so good. I took a fat slice of egg bread and put real butter on it. It was better than cake.

"Just one piece of bread," said my mom.

"He shouldn't have any," Dad said.

Grandma looked at both of my parents. "His first meal home," she said. "He's entitled."

"He's got a long way to go," Dad said.

"He'll get there, don't worry," said Grandma.

"Not without help," Dad said. "Rose, you've got to cooperate. Ned can't do it by himself."

"Please," Grandma said. "He's just a growing boy and you're all making such a fuss out of it. Is it a crime to make something he likes?" She stood up and started clearing plates from the table. Mom helped her. In a little while she wheeled in the cart with dessert and when I saw it, my heart jumped up. There was a big, delicious-looking chocolate cake. And on top, Grandma had written WELCOME HOME NEDDIE in white script.

"Grandma!" I said. "It's beautiful!"

"Of course," she nodded. "For my own Neddie, only the best." She cut a big slice and served me first. It felt as if it was my birthday.

The cake was great, and so was the big glass of milk

that went with it. I had forgotten how good milk is. Real milk, I mean, not that rotten blue milk they gave us in camp. I wanted another slice of cake, but I knew I shouldn't have it. So I took another glass of milk instead.

Dad didn't have any cake. He just stirred his coffee and looked over the table at me. "How much do you weigh now?" he asked.

"A hundred and four."

Dad took a sip of his coffee. "Not anymore," he said slowly, "not anymore."

20

The next morning Dad was sitting and reading the newspaper when I came down to breakfast. "Right after breakfast I want to weigh you," he said.

"Oh, no, you don't," I said. "Let's do it before I eat."

Dad grinned and got up to follow me upstairs. "What are you doing?" he asked when I started taking off my shirt.

"I'm not getting weighed all dressed again," I said. I took off my sneakers and then my pants. Then I took off my socks and underpants. "This is the way I weigh myself," I said. "Naked, and in the morning before breakfast." I stepped onto the scale, letting my toes kind of curl over the front edge.

"Toes on the scale," Dad said, and when I made a face he said, "come on." He bent down and read the scale. "One hundred and five pounds."

"Nuts," I said. "I must have gained a pound."

"After that dinner last night, I'm not surprised."

Dad sat down on the toilet seat while I got dressed again. "I've got a question for you, Ned. Do you really want to lose weight?"

"Sure."

"Really?" Dad said. "In your heart of hearts do you truly want to lose weight?"

"Yes," I said.

Dad thought about that for a few moments. "Okay, then. Next question. How do you propose going about it?"

I shrugged. "I'll eat less."

"Starting when?" Dad asked.

"Soon," I said. "Maybe today."

"Maybe?"

"How about when school starts?"

"You could weigh what you did before you went to camp by then," Dad said. "Ned, I'd hate to see you put back the weight you lost over the summer. You did well up at camp. You lost fourteen pounds, which is excellent. You mustn't start backsliding."

"What's backsliding?" It sounded like a way of going downhill in the snow.

"Going back to your old habits," Dad said. "I can't let you do that."

"I won't," I said, but I guess I didn't sound too sure.

"Look," Dad said, "I don't want the whole family going crazy over your diet, and I don't want to make you insane either. We've got to have a plan and we've got to stick to it. It's the only way, Ned."

"Okay," I said.

Dad thought for a few minutes, sitting there not saying anything. Then he got up. "Come into Mom's office," he said, and I followed him down the hall. He picked up the calendar from Mom's desk. "Look, Ned, suppose we try this. I'll make a note on the calendar of what you weighed today. Then every week, we'll do the same thing, okay? This way, we'll have a record of how you're doing. What's today?"

"Saturday."

Dad wrote 105 pounds on the calendar next to the date. Then he turned back to the day I went off to camp and wrote 116 pounds there. "According to my scale, you lost eleven pounds at camp, not fourteen," he said, "but never mind. The important thing is that you keep losing. I'd like to see what you look like at seventy-five pounds."

"Yipes!" I said. "That means I have to lose thirty pounds more!"

"You can do it, Ned."

"Sure, in about two years."

Dad laughed. Then he got serious. "I'll make a deal with you. What would you like as a reward for losing the weight you're supposed to lose?"

I thought for a moment. There really wasn't anything I could think of that I wanted that bad.

Dad looked at the calendar again. "Tell you what," he said, "suppose we start planning now for Christmas vacation. That's far enough off to give you enough time to lose thirty pounds."

"I think we better make it Easter vacation," I said.

"Okay," Dad said, smiling, "you're the boss. Easter vacation it is. Lose thirty pounds by Easter, and we'll all go on a trip. Let's say . . . Disney World."

"Great!" I said. Last Christmas, Steve Adolphus and his family went to Disney World and they had a fantastic time.

"Now a deal is a deal," Dad said. "Thirty pounds, Ned, or no vacation." He stuck out his hand and we shook on it. "I think we're going to have a lot of fun in Disney World next spring," he said.

I, on the other hand, kind of doubted we'd even get to go.

21

What is there about the beginning of school each fall that makes you feel so awful?

I have never figured out why I always get that feeling in my stomach the night before school begins (and maybe for a whole *week* before that) because I never let anything connected with school get into my head during the summer.

But every September there comes that same feeling again, like a heavy overcoat that weighs you down and down. You know that everything is going to be different once school begins. You can't stay up late at night anymore. You can't play ball all day long, or just spend a day hanging around if you want to. You have to start paying attention to things like wearing neat clothes, and are your fingernails clipped, and what is the exact state of cleanliness of your ears. And you know those Sunday nights when it's so hard to fall asleep are going to begin all over again.

Grandma had a surprise present for me on the morning when school began. It was an official National Football League lunchbox, with emblems on it of all the teams. "I thought you'd like it," she said, after I'd kissed her. She looked at me for a second, judging the clothes I was wearing, which were my new corduroy jeans and a clean long-sleeve shirt. "A beautiful boy," she said, then gave me a hug as I went out the door. "Pay attention to the teacher!" she called after me. My grandma is from what she calls "the old school." It means that she thinks the teacher is always right—no matter what.

Steve Adolphus was waiting in front of his house down the street. We were walking to school together, like always. Steve had had a great summer in Camp Sha-Kah-Na-Kee. There were three kids we knew from the year before in his bunk, and they all asked for me. And Steve's softball team won their league, and were on the winning side in color war, too. That was the summer I should have had, instead of stupid Camp Lean-Too.

"I wonder what Mister Pangalos is going to be like?" Steve said. We were at the last crossing before school. Mr. Pangalos was our teacher this year.

"I heard he was okay," I said.

"I heard he was strict."

"Thanks a lot," I said to Steve. That was not the kind of talk I liked to hear on the first day of school.

It turned out that Mr. Pangalos was both okay and kind of strict. If you did your work, he was okay. If you goofed around, he could eat your ears for breakfast. I managed to sit right next to Steve and Libby Klein, which was the way I'd hoped it would work out.

We had early lunch this year, and we got to the lunch room at eleven thirty. When I opened my new lunchbox, I got a surprise. Grandma had gone bonkers about my lunch. There were *two* sandwiches for me, not one, plus two doughnuts, chocolate milk, and a banana. The sandwiches were sliced chicken, my favorite, made on thick slices of egg bread, spread with butter and just a touch of mayonnaise. In ordinary days, I would eat everything in my lunchbox in about two minutes flat. But today was no ordinary day.

As I sat there in the noisy lunchroom looking into my new lunchbox that she had just given me, I knew that I had to do something about Grandma if I wasn't going to go back to Camp Lean-Too next summer. I don't know why everything came clear to me at that exact moment, but it did.

There was too much food in my lunchbox.

There was too much food in my home.

There was too much food *in my whole life!*

And a very important reason for too much food was my grandmother. She was too good to me. She wanted to feed me until I was all fattened up for Camp Lean-Too again. But I was not going to let her do it. I would do anything not to go back to Camp Lean-Too again. And if it meant hurting Grandma, then I would have to hurt her.

I opened both sandwiches and just ate the chicken. I

117

left all of Grandma's wonderful egg bread. I took a few sips of my chocolate milk, then forgot about the rest. I took both doughnuts and handed one to Libby and one to Steve.

"Are you sick or something?" Steve asked.

"No."

"You never give away doughnuts," Libby said.

"You are looking at the new Nathaniel Robbins. From now on, I am on a diet."

"Sure you are," Steve said, nodding. He'd heard me say that before.

"This time, I really mean it," I said. I felt great. So full of confidence and a kind of strength. "You'll see," I said. "I am going to lose weight. Really, I am. I am going to be a normal person."

Just as I said that, I saw a hand reach over my shoulder and into my lunchbox. "Jelly Belly!" Phil Steinkraus said, taking my banana. He gave me a rap on the top of my head with his knuckles. "How ya doin', fatso?"

I looked up at him. "Terrific," I said. It's amazing how you can talk to a person you hate and not let on that you do.

Phil reached over and snatched at the doughnut I had just given to Libby, but she was too quick for him. She held the doughnut away from him with one hand and elbowed Phil right in the belly. "Get lost, bird-brain," she said.

Phil kind of snickered under his breath, but he did walk away.

Steve and I looked at each other. "How'd you do that, Libby?" Steve asked.

"Do what?"

"Talk back to Phil Steinkraus without getting slaughtered."

Libby grinned. "I'm not afraid of him," she said.

"Well," Steve said, "you're a girl."

"What difference does that make?" Libby said. "Phil Steinkraus is a jerk. He once tried to grab my lunchbox away from me on the bus and I hit him on the head with it."

Steve looked at me and shrugged. "We're both afraid of him," I said to Libby.

She looked at us like we were some kind of weird Martians. "Afraid of Phil Steinkraus?" She laughed. "That's the funniest thing I ever heard."

"Libby," I said, "if I tangled with Phil Steinkraus he would kill me."

"Well," she said, "why don't you try it once and find out?"

Which was easy for her to say. I, on the other hand, didn't care if I never found out.

22

When I walked home that afternoon my mind was about a half-mile ahead of me. Steve was chattering about Mr. Pangalos, what kind of school supplies he would buy, the book reports we would have to write, but I hardly heard him. I was thinking about Grandma.

I told myself I would just march right into the house and say that I didn't want to be fattened up anymore. I would tell her to stop baking such wonderful bread and cakes and cookies. To stop stuffing my lunchbox every day. To quit giving me those huge portions of mashed potatoes, orange French toast, and all the other things I had learned to love.

To tell you the truth, I was scared.

I knew I had to say all those things to Grandma. But I also knew she would be hurt.

When I walked into the house, Grandma was waiting in the kitchen. "Jamie telephoned from school," she said. "He wants you to do him a favor and bring over all his track things."

I was relieved. I raced upstairs, gathered Jamie's running gear, and put it in his Adidas bag. Then I came back down to the kitchen.

"So how was school?" Grandma asked.

"Good. I better get going. If Jamie called, he must need his things quick."

"Slow yourself down a minute," Grandma said. "Have a glass of milk, a cookie . . ."

"I better get my bike," I said. I gave Grandma a quick kiss and dashed out the back door.

"Be careful," she called after me, "and watch out for cars."

Jamie was doing his stretching exercises on the infield of the track when I got to Wilson High. "Coach called a quick practice," he said as he pushed his forehead down to meet his knee. "I thought we wouldn't start training till next week." Jamie looked worried.

Members of the track team, all wearing their Wilson High shirts, were circling the quarter mile cinder track. Down at the far end of the field the football squad was running pass patterns. Two husky track men came loping by. "Get with it, Robbins!" one of them called.

"Lynn and Covelli," Jamie said. "They've put in an hour already, and I haven't even started." He got up from the ground, took his track bag, and went inside to the locker room to change. I put my bike into the rack outside the door, then walked down to sit in the bleachers. After a while, Jamie came out of the locker room. I saw him talking to the track coach, Mr. Samuels, then he came jogging over. "Want to keep me company while I warm up?" he asked.

"Sure," I said. I joined him on the track and we both started jogging. "Now go slow," I said.

"Very slow, squirt," Jamie grinned. "At least till I get warm."

We jogged down the long straightaway of the track side by side. It felt terrific to be actually running with my brother.

"Coach laid it out for me," Jamie said. "I'm going to have to show him something or I can forget about cross-country."

"But you want cross-country, don't you?"

Jamie did a few hopping steps while I jogged on. He had no trouble keeping up with me. "That I do," he said. "But I'll have to outrun Lynn and Covelli. And to outrun them, I'll have to out-train them. It's as simple as that."

We came to the turn in the track and I felt good. "Running is neat," I said.

"A bit boring, but fun," Jamie said. He began lifting his knees high, still keeping pace with me. "If those guys run one hour, I'll have to run two. If they do two hours, I'll do three."

"You really want it," I said.

"I want it. And I'm going to have it." Jamie grinned at me. "It's all inside, Neddie. Right in your guts. Runners don't beat other runners in races. They beat themselves. By running farther and faster than they

think they possibly can. When a guy wins a race, he's winning a victory over himself."

I was beginning to lose my breath and I started to slow down.

"I've got a plan," Jamie said. "Out here, after school, I'll match Lynn and Covelli's training hours. But at home, after dinner in the evenings . . ." He winked at me.

"You'll do your extra training."

"That's the plan," Jamie said. "We have a meet in October. I think Mr. Lynn and Mr. Covelli will have a surprise waiting for them."

"I think you'll do it," I said, gasping, "but I won't." I was out of breath, and my legs were beginning to feel very heavy. "Better slow down."

"Come on," Jamie said, "you can do a quarter mile at this pace, can't you? One turn around the track."

I groaned, but I jogged on with Jamie. We came around the far turn and there was only a short distance to the spot where we had begun. I didn't know how I had the strength to drag myself there, but I didn't want to show my brother I couldn't. I made it.

"Now just keep walking till you get your breath back," Jamie said, then he took off. I watched him get to the near turn in what seemed like just a few strides. Jamie was a beautiful runner, with a long-legged, very easy motion. It seemed as if he was putting no effort into it, but I knew how fast he could fly.

When I reached the turn, Jamie had run a full lap. He slowed as he reached me, jogging in place. "One more lap for you," he said, "and six for me."

"I can't run anymore," I protested.

"Sure you can," Jamie said, "try it." He zoomed off again.

I walked and walked until I had my breath back, then began jogging again. And Jamie was right. The second lap was easier than the first one.

I waited in the bleachers while Jamie finished his six laps, then watched while he did three more at a very fast pace. When Jamie wants something, he really goes after it.

"A good start," Jamie said as he toweled off. "For both of us," he added.

"I'm no runner," I said.

"Not yet, Neddie. But you could be. I think it would help you with your weight problem."

"Someone else has to help me with my weight problem," I said. "Grandma."

Jamie looked out at me from under his towel. "So you've finally gotten there," he said.

"I've got to speak to her."

"Yes, you do," Jamie said.

"She's going to be angry. And maybe hurt."

"Uh-huh," Jamie nodded, "she will."

"But I've got to do it," I said.

Jamie put a hand on my shoulder. "Neddie," he said, "for the first time, I really believe you truly want to lose weight."

"Now what I have to do," I said, "is convince Grandma."

23

"I don't feel too hungry today," I told Grandma the next morning, "so don't give me two sandwiches for lunch."

I had already turned down Grandma's pancakes and was eating a bowl of the protein cereal flakes Dad likes.

"Are you okay?" Grandma asked. She came walking over and put a hand on my forehead. "Cool," she said.

"I'm fine," I said. Before we could say more Elizabeth came rushing into the kitchen for breakfast, followed by Mom. Mornings in our kitchen are not a good time for long conversations. With five of us having breakfast, going off to school and work, and Grandma packing lunches for Elizabeth and me, it's a pretty busy place.

So I didn't actually know what was in my lunchbox until I sat down in the lunchroom with Steve and

Libby and opened it. There were two thick sandwiches of Grandma's meatloaf, a slice of chocolate cake, a tomato, a banana, and a Thermos of chocolate milk.

"What kind of diet are you on, anyway?" Steve asked, as he gazed into my lunchbox.

"A Jelly Belly diet," Libby said.

"I'm on a diet," I said, "only Grandma doesn't know it yet." I took the two sandwiches out of my lunchbox. "I asked her to give me only one sandwich," I said.

"Sure you did," Steve smirked.

"And I didn't have pancakes this morning," I said.

Libby laughed and I could see she didn't believe me. "Well," she said to Steve, "I didn't have mashed potatoes this morning."

"And I didn't have spaghetti," Steve answered her.

"I didn't have any french fries for breakfast," Libby said.

"And I didn't have a Big Mac," Steve said.

By now the both of them were cracking up. "Okay, you guys," I said, "cut it out." I unwrapped one of my sandwiches and ate only the meat part, along with some of my milk. That was really all I was going to eat, but I was still hungry. I ate the meat from the other sandwich, too. "Anyone want some empty bread?" I asked.

"No," said Libby, "but I'll take that banana."

"And I'll take your chocolate cake," Steve said. He

licked off the thick icing and left the cake. "Great," he said. "I love your diet."

"Yeah," Libby said, "tell your grandma I'd like some cookies tomorrow."

By the time school was over I was starving. But I was determined to have it out with Grandma.

When I walked in the front door, I almost went right out again. The house smelled like heaven. I put my books down and went into the kitchen. "What is that great smell?" I asked. But even as I asked I could see the answer, cooling on two racks near the oven. Grandma's special peanut butter cookies. "Oh, God!" I exclaimed.

"Some are already cool," Grandma said. "Have a few, with some milk."

"A few!" I could probably have eaten all of them with no trouble at all. Instead, I went to the fruit bowl and took an apple. "Grandma, I've got to talk to you," I said.

"Why not." She was putting cookie dough onto a metal sheet with a teaspoon.

"I have to lose weight, Grandma. I'm too fat."

"Nonsense," she said. She turned away and put the cookie sheet into the oven.

"I eat too much," I said.

"You eat like a growing boy."

"I weigh a hundred and five pounds," I said. "It's too much."

"You have big bones," she said, "like me. It runs in our family."

"The doctor's chart says I should weigh seventy-five."

"Chart, shmart," she said. "You can't go by some chart that was thought up by a few skinny people." She put three cookies on a plate and set it down on the table. "Have some milk," she said.

"Grandma," I said, "I'm talking but you're not listening."

"Who's not listening?" She sat down at the table and I did, too. Before I could say anything more she pushed the plate of cookies to me. "Have a cookie, you'll feel better," she said.

"*Grandma!*" I exploded. "You haven't heard a single word I said!"

Behind her steel-rimmed eyeglasses she blinked at me. "Like that you talk to a grandma?" she said in a hurt voice.

"I'm sorry," I said, "but here I am, talking about something serious, and you give me cookies."

"Is that a crime?" she shrugged. "To give something good to a boy I love?"

"Yes!" I said, much too loud and forceful. "It's wrong. Everything you do in this kitchen is wrong! You're making me into a freak!"

Grandma sat very still, looking at me.

"You've got to stop all this cooking and baking," I said.

Grandma drew her lips into a tight line. "You think it's easy, feeding a family like ours?" she said.

"Grandma—"

129

"It's a full-time job, let me tell you, my little Neddie. But I cook and I bake to make you all feel good and keep you happy. You don't remember what a skinny *marink* you were when I first moved into this house. Like a ghost, you looked. I could see every bone sticking out."

"And look at me now!" I jumped up and stuck my stomach out, then turned to show her my fat butt. "Fat, fat, fat!"

Grandma shook her head. "Don't worry about it, Neddie. You'll see, soon you'll shoot up like a weed and you'll be just right."

"I won't!" I shouted. "Not if you keep stuffing me this way!"

"If you knew what pleasure it gives me to see you eat," she said. "You were so skinny . . ."

"But I'm not now! I hate myself this way!"

"In my eyes, you're not fat," Grandma said. "And that's all I want to hear about it." She got up from the table and went to the oven.

"You're no help at all!" I shouted at her. "Cookies and doughnuts and bread and cake and two sandwiches for lunch! You've made me into a pig, Grandma! A big fat pig!"

I never saw the look in Grandma's eyes that I saw now. I thought she was going to hit me. "Apologize, Nathaniel," she said.

"I will not! It's true, and you know it!"

"Apologize!" she commanded.

"No!"

130

Grandma nodded once and looked right past me. "From now on," she said, "we don't talk. Not another word until you apologize."

"I won't!"

Grandma turned her back. "I don't talk to pigs," she said.

24

I ran upstairs to my room and for once in my life I didn't cry. Maybe because I was so angry. I wanted Grandma to help—*needed* her to help me, in fact—if I was going to lose weight. And when I finally got up the courage to talk to her about it, she was turning her back on me. It was unfair.

I had a ton of homework. Mr. Pangalos believed in it, which did not make him my favorite teacher in the whole world. But I was too upset to sit down and start working. So I changed into a pair of shorts and a T-shirt, and put on my sneakers. I was going over to Wilson High to run again.

I sneaked out of the house quietly, not telling Grandma where I was going like I was supposed to do. If I wasn't talking to her, I figured, then I wasn't telling her *that*, either.

Jamie was running hard around the track when I put my bike in the rack. He waved and kept on going.

I jogged out on the track and began doing a lap. Just running started to make me feel better. Calmer, somehow, and more in control of myself.

When Jamie finished his lap he jogged alongside me while I told him about my fight with Grandma. One thing about Jamie, he's a good listener.

"Grandma can be very stubborn," Jamie said, which made me smile because that's the same thing Dad often says about Grandma. "And blowing your top was not a good idea," he added.

"But she made me so mad! She wouldn't even listen!"

"Stay cool, fool," Jamie said, "and slow down."

I hadn't realized it, but in telling him about Grandma I had started to run a little faster than a jog.

"See if you can do two laps at this slow pace without stopping," Jamie said, and he ran off to take one more hard lap. I kept jogging along, finished one lap, and started another. Halfway around it I thought my lungs would burst, but I kept going. When I finished my second lap, Jamie was walking with me. "How do you feel?" he asked.

"Good." I really did.

"Okay. Walk until you get your breath back, then take another lap."

"You're kidding," I said. "I'll die."

"Save your breath, Ned, and do what I say. You're loose now and it won't be hard. Try it."

I walked a half-length of the track and then started

jogging again. Jamie was right. I did another lap with no trouble at all.

"You just jogged three-quarters of a mile," Jamie said. "You have the makings of a runner, squirt, no kidding."

"Can I run with you tonight? After dinner?"

"No," Jamie said, "that's too much. But if you come out here every day, I think you can be doing a mile at a good pace in no time."

I waited while Jamie finished his training, then he gave me a ride home on the handlebars of my bike. "What'll I do about Grandma, Jamie?"

"You'll have to make peace with her, that's for sure."

"But how?"

"You could start by apologizing."

Grandma was working in the kitchen when we got home. I knew she had seen me walk in, but she made believe she didn't. "Grandma," I said.

"I'm busy cooking dinner," she said. "Which some people in this house appreciate, even though others don't." And then she turned her back on me. Again.

I took a shower and settled down to my homework. I had to read a chapter in my social studies book about the Ice Age. As I read it, I couldn't help thinking that a new kind of Ice Age had started between Grandma and me.

Dinner was a very strange meal. It was as if Grandma was showing off for me by serving some of her very special foods. Especially the ones she knew I liked. There were crispy fish cakes, spaghetti with her special sauce, and an egg bread even though it wasn't Friday. And, of course, peanut butter cookies so sweet and chewy and kind of melty in your mouth.

But if Grandma wanted to make me love her again by eating like a pig, she was using the wrong scheme. No more would I eat until my belly ached. The days of stuffing myself were gone.

It's funny how you can be so hungry—and boy, was I hungry—and yet if you have that diet feeling going good, you can resist overeating. All I had eaten so far this day was that cereal in the morning, the meat from my sandwiches, some milk, and an apple. And yet I could control myself. I ate two carrot sticks, one fish-cake, a very small amount of spaghetti, no bread and no cookies. My dessert was a glass of milk.

Dad looked at my dinner plate and noticed that I had left one fishcake and most of the spaghetti. "Not hungry, Ned?" he asked.

"No. I guess I had enough."

He winked at me.

Grandma was very quiet, but I saw her looking at me.

"It was delicious," I said to her.

"Good," she said.

"Like it always is."

Grandma nodded and looked away. The Ice Age was continuing.

Let me tell you something. I loved my grandma as much as anyone else in my family (if not more).

And seeing her ignore me the way she was, that hurt. A lot.

I guess I was thinking about that, and some other things, as I lay in bed. There are some nights when you just can't turn off your mind, and this was one of them. I thought about all the good things Grandma had done for me since she moved into the house. I remembered the days when I was little and she would walk me to the school bus in the mornings. And how I felt holding her hand in the street. Not like a baby, but kind of proud.

I remembered the day I cut my hand badly on a piece of glass, and how she had wrapped my hand in a towel and rushed me off to the hospital. And how she sat holding me while the doctor put five stitches into the cut to close it.

I remembered the new catcher's mitt I wanted and how my Dad said I should wait until next year for it, because my old mitt was still good. And how Grandma took me off to the store after school and bought that new mitt for me. She was so funny, trying to talk baseball with me and not knowing the first thing about it.

I lay in bed thinking of how, on rainy days when everyone else was busy, Grandma would always find time to sit at the kitchen table with me and play rummy. It took me a while to catch on, but I finally realized that she purposely threw away cards she needed, so I would always win.

And the more I thought about Grandma, the worse

I felt. I couldn't sleep. I looked at the digital clock on my dresser and saw that it was one seventeen in the morning. I was wide awake. I put on my bathrobe and went down to the kitchen.

Grandma was sitting at the table, a cup of tea in front of her. She was reading the evening newspaper. She turned to look at me as I entered the kitchen, then glanced back at her paper.

I went to the refrigerator, poured myself a glass of milk, then sat down at the table next to her. "I couldn't sleep," I said.

"Hmmm," she said, kind of to herself. She turned a page in the newspaper.

"Grandma . . . I didn't mean to yell at you that way."

She looked right past me at the wall. "Do I hear a voice?" she said. She turned her head to look at the refrigerator. "Could be I heard a voice, but so far it didn't say those words I'm waiting to hear."

"I apologize, Grandma. I'm sorry."

"Aha!" Grandma said. "I'm beginning to recognize that voice."

"It's me . . . Neddie."

"I do know that person," Grandma said. She looked at me from behind her eyeglasses. "You're the same one who marched in here after school and told me I was feeding a pig, right?"

"I apologize," I repeated. "I can't blame you for making me fat. Because I was the one who did the eating."

Grandma's lips twitched. "That's better," she said. "You don't know how that hurt me . . . telling me that everything I did for five years was all wrong."

"Grandma," I said, "I love you. I didn't mean to hurt you." I got up and put my arms around her, then gave her a kiss. She grabbed me and moaned a little, then hugged me tight. "Light of my life," she said, and I don't know why but I started crying. And she was crying, too, and the both of us rocked a little in each other's arms.

Grandma took a tissue out of her pocket and blew her nose. "Look at me, a real weeping Willie," she said. She cleared her throat. "We must never get so angry with each other, Neddie, because I can't stand it. Will you promise me that?"

"I promise." I sat down next to her and we held hands.

"All right, Rose," she said to herself, "enough with the waterworks." She wiped her eyes with a tissue. "Now then," she went on, "what are we going to do with you?"

"Help me, Grandma. I don't want to be fat any-more. I hate it."

"If you get too skinny, so help me I'll kill you."

"I won't," I said. "I just want to weigh seventy-five pounds."

"We'll see," Grandma said. "No more cakes and cookies. You know that?"

"Yes. And no more stuffed lunchboxes, either."

"Right. No more a lot of things, Neddie." She looked at the glass of milk standing on the table.

"Cold milk you're drinking? Let me at least warm it up for you."

"I hate warm milk."

"I'll just take the chill off." She took the glass of milk, went to the stove, and poured it into a pan. "Your grandpa, he should rest, he was a heavy man all his life, too. And I learned a few things about dieting from feeding him."

"You know, Grandma," I said, "if I get down to seventy-five pounds by Easter, Dad is going to take all of us to Disney World."

"Wonderful," she said. "Can you see an old lady like me in Disney World?" She laughed.

"Of course," I said. "It'll be fun. And you're not an old lady."

Grandma laughed again, and brought back the glass of milk to me. It tasted awful, but I sipped it anyway.

"You want a cookie?" she asked, but I could see by her face she was joking.

"Of course. But I'm not going to have one."

She pinched my cheek. "Good boy," she said. "Now then, if I was the one who made you fat, I'll be the one to make you skinny . . ." She began walking slowly to the refrigerator, talking to herself. "Let's see . . . I'll cut down on the baking . . . and the starchy foods . . ."

She looked so funny walking up and down, talking to herself, that I wanted to laugh. Instead I said, "Grandma, I love you."

She smiled at me. "Let's see if you'll still say that after you see your lunchbox tomorrow."

25

Grandma almost overdid it.

When I opened my lunchbox the next day at school, this is what I found. Two hard-boiled eggs, a small tomato, four carrot sticks, a thin slice of egg bread with no butter on it, a little salt shaker, a Thermos of milk, and a note.

I opened the note. "THINK SKINNY!" it said, in Grandma's printing. It made me smile.

"That is a stupid lunch," Libby said.

"No, it isn't," I said, "that is a very smart lunch."

"No cookies? No cake?" Steve wanted to know.

"Zip-o," I said.

"You're just no fun at lunch anymore," Steve sighed.

I discovered something while eating lunch. Hard boiled eggs can fill you up, and they don't taste too bad with salt on them. And the tomato was good, too. It was amazing how little I could eat and still feel good.

That night at dinner, we all talked about it. "What's

happened," Dad said, "is that your stomach has shrunk."

"It's still too big," Elizabeth said in her nasty way.

"Thanks," I said, and stuck my tongue out at her.

"The stomach is able to expand and contract, depending on how much food you put in it," Dad went on. "By eating less, you've made it smaller. So it doesn't take as much food to fill it up. You feel satisfied eating less now, and that's good."

I'll say it was good. You might not believe this, but I ate a peach for dessert that night and I could hardly finish it.

My stomach was probably no bigger than a peanut.

"I don't believe it," my Dad said. He bent down again to look at the scale. "It's correct. Ninety-eight pounds, Ned!"

"Holy Toledo!" I said.

"You've lost seven pounds in a week."

It was a pretty amazing figure. Seven pounds in one week. Why that was half of what I lost in a whole summer at Camp Lean-Too. And I hadn't even curled my toes over the front of the scale!

I got dressed again and followed Dad down to Saturday breakfast. "I have an announcement to make," Dad said.

Jamie put a hand to his mouth and blew a kind of fanfare.

"Thank you," Dad said. "Ladies and gentlemen, I have the honor to announce that in the very first week of his diet, my son, Nathaniel Robbins, has lost a grand total of . . ."

Dad paused to make it dramatic and Jamie blew another fanfare.

". . . Seven pounds!"

Grandma "oohed," Mom "aahed," and everyone began to applaud. I was a little embarrassed, but I took a funny bow, anyway.

"Congratulations," Jamie said, and we shook hands.

"And special for you this morning, to celebrate," said Grandma, "pancakes!"

I looked to see if Grandma was joking, but she was serious.

"You know I can't have pancakes," I said.

"Trust me," Grandma grinned. She poured some pale batter on the griddle. "I found the recipe in one of my ladies' magazines. It's practically all cottage cheese, which is very low in calories. And I put in a little honey so you won't need pancake syrup."

They really weren't too bad. On the other hand, they weren't too good, either. But with a glass of milk they filled me up.

"I'm really proud of you, Neddie," Mom said. "But don't start thinking you can lose seven pounds every week."

"Why not?" It was exactly what I was thinking. In about another month at this rate I'd be down to my proper weight.

"It doesn't work that way, darling," Mom said. "Every person dieting loses the biggest amount in the

142

first week. I guess because the body has the most to lose then. But it gets harder as you go along, and you'll lose less each week."

"That's unfair," I said.

"Life is unfair," Dad said.

"You mean it's going to take me more than a month to get down to seventy-five pounds?"

"We'll see, Neddie," said Mom, "we'll see."

26

It actually took more than six months.

And there were a lot of bad times along the way. Days when I was ready to give anything up for just one candy bar. Those afternoons when I'd come home from school starving and Grandma would be baking something terrific and my mouth would water. Thank heavens for Grandma. She always had a glass of milk ready for me, to cut my hunger. Or there were a couple of crackers spread with cottage cheese and cinnamon. One of the hardest times was when we had company for dinner, and I would have to sit there watching everyone stuff themselves with cakes and pies while I munched on an apple and said, "Oh, no thank you—I'm on a diet."

But what a good feeling it was on those Saturday mornings when I'd weigh in and Dad would write down the figures on Mom's calendar.

SEPT. 28—95
OCT. 10—92
OCT. 17—89
OCT. 24—88

And then there were those weeks when I didn't lose a pound. They were the hardest weeks of all. But with everybody helping, and running my bad feelings away on the track with Jamie, I got through them.

The times I wanted to forget my diet and go eat a bear, fur and all, were when things were going bad. I goofed up a test or lost a book or just got out of bed on the wrong side that morning. What I did on those days was gobble a lot of my *hate* foods. Things I could bite on real hard, so I got my anger out of me. Carrot sticks, apples, green pepper, and even the dreaded celery stalk. Something hard to chew on that kind of chews back.

Grandma's notes in my lunchbox helped a lot. I kept some of them and put them on the cork board above my desk. Like this one:

SKINNINESS IS IN THE MIND—FATNESS IS IN THE MOUTH

Right about then, when I had lost a good amount of weight, I began to do some nutty things.

Like sucking in my gut in front of people so I looked extra skinny. And in the mornings, when I brushed my teeth, sometimes I'd pull my cheeks in and make skinny, monkey faces at myself. I was getting weird.

Another thing I did was strip down to my underpants and pose in front of the mirror on my closet door. Between the diet and running with Jamie, I was getting to look like a person instead of a blob. I sucked everything in and tried to make my muscles bulge out. I posed like Lou Ferrigno, the Incredible Hulk. It wasn't even close. I was still Nat Robbins, the Incredible Bulk.

But I was getting there.

27

On the last Saturday in October, the whole family went to see Jamie run in his meet. It was a raw, cold day and Jamie looked like he was freezing in his shorts and running shirt. But when the gun went off in the two-mile race, he warmed up quick. He was out in front the whole race and finished in his best time ever, winning by about ten yards.

This was in the morning. Just after lunch, we all went over to the park where the six-mile cross-country race would be run. It was what Jamie had been spending all those extra night-time hours training for.

The finish of the race was on a straightaway on top of a hill. We could see the runners all strung out down below as they came to this last and very steep hill. And there was Jamie, with about five runners in front of him, coming to the bottom of the hill. And both Lynn and Covelli were in front of him. He looked very tired, and why not—he had covered about six miles by now—and two miles in his morning race. But he caught up with Lynn on the hill and passed him, and then he passed two more guys from Taft High, and when he reached the top of the hill there was only Covelli in front.

But Jamie didn't make it. He tried to run faster, but he just couldn't pass Covelli. Jamie finished second in the cross-country race.

After dinner, we took a walk around the neighborhood. For one night at least, Jamie wasn't training. He hadn't said much after the race, but I could tell he was disappointed. "You must feel terrible," I said when we had rounded the corner.

"Oh, I don't know," Jamie said. "Last spring I couldn't even make the cross-country squad. Now I'm number two."

"But you wanted to be number one, right?"

"Yes, I did," Jamie said. "But, Neddie, I started training very late. I goofed off all summer, don't forget, and Covelli didn't. So maybe he deserves to be number one after all."

"But aren't you disappointed?"

Jamie laughed and squeezed my shoulder with his big hand. "You bet I'm disappointed, squirt," he said, "but what good does that do? I did my best and I finished second. Okay, next case. The big meets are in the spring. Who knows what will happen in the spring?"

I knew what would happen in the spring all right. We were not going to Disney World. Because I got stuck on seventy-nine pounds and couldn't lose another ounce.

28

Seventy-nine pounds seemed to be the bottom limit for me. I got down to that weight in January and I couldn't get away from it. Week after week, Saturday after Saturday, the same figure was written down on the calendar.

"Does this mean we won't go to Disney World?" I asked Dad when for the fifth week in a row I weighed the same.

"A deal is a deal, Neddie," he said. "We agreed on seventy-five pounds, didn't we?"

"Yes."

Dad looked at me and shrugged. "Four pounds to go," he said.

Four rotten pounds, after all the weight I'd lost, and it looked as if I'd never lose them. It was an awful blow after I'd worked so hard and so long. But Dad was strict about agreements. It was like a contract, he always said, and contracts were his business.

I felt so bad I wanted to cry. But I didn't. It was just

one of those disappointments that you just have to get over. But one day in February I went with Mom to see Dr. Brandt for my annual checkup.

Dr. Brandt was amazed at the way I looked. "Is this the same Nathaniel I saw last year?" he asked my mom.

"No," I answered for her. "That was Jelly Belly. He's gone. What I am now is Normal Nathaniel."

"I should say so," Dr. Brandt said. "You look terrific. I guess that special summer camp we talked about did the trick," he said to Mom.

That was the first time I found out that Dr. Brandt was the one who suggested I be sent to Camp Lean-Too in the first place.

"The camp helped a little," Mom said, "but the hardest part Ned did all on his own."

"Well," said Dr. Brandt, "you should be very proud of yourself, Nathaniel."

Not too proud, I said to myself. I'm four pounds short of being really proud, and going to Disney World, too.

Dr. Brandt did all of his doctor things to me. Looked in my eyes and my ears and even up my nose. Poked and prodded and heard my chest as I breathed in and out. He weighed me and measured my height. Seventy-nine pounds was what I weighed, even on his scale. And he took that little pin and stuck my finger with it, then got a drop of my blood on this card. I always hate that part of his examination.

When he was all through, the three of us sat down in his office. "He's fine," Dr. Brandt said to Mom.

"But the best part of it is that he is exactly on target in the weight department."

I didn't think I heard him right. "No, I'm not," I said. "I'm supposed to be seventy-five pounds and I'm seventy-nine pounds. I still have to lose four pounds."

"You're forgetting something, Nathaniel," said Dr. Brandt.

"I am?"

"Your *height*. You've grown an inch and a half since your checkup last year . . ."

"I have?"

Dr. Brandt chuckled. "You are now just about the perfect weight for your height, Nathaniel. In fact, according to my chart, you could even *gain* a pound or two."

Wow, wow, and double wow! Flashing skyrockets shot off in my head and I wanted to jump up and kiss the doctor. I didn't, of course. But what I did do was leap in the air and yell at the top of my voice. Then I hugged and kissed Mom.

"I'm so proud of you," she said.

"I'm kind of proud of me, too," I said, grinning like an idiot.

"I guess we can make those reservations now," Mom said.

"*All right!*" I said. I had made it after all!

29

There's really only a couple of things left to tell.

Dad made reservations for our trip to Disney World. We were going to stay in the Contemporary Hotel, right inside the park. And there was a monorail that went right *through* the lobby of our hotel. I couldn't wait for Easter vacation.

It was a very wet spring, with rain almost every day. Especially on school days. Grandma got mad at me a lot for walking to and from school all the time. And coming home soaked.

I guess I got mad at myself, too. The only reason I didn't take the school bus was that stupid Phil Steinkraus. Libby laughed at Steve and me. She said we were chicken, and nutty, too, because Phil Steinkraus was just a lot of big talk. "Blow on him and he'll fall down," she said.

So one rainy morning when I picked Steve up at his house, I said we should take the bus. "What about Phil Steinkraus?" Steve asked.

"I'll be right behind you," I said. "If he starts anything, I'll help you."

"That's very nice of you," Steve said.

"I'm a very nice person," I said. "Especially since I got skinny."

"And I suppose if I'm bleeding, you'll help bandage me," Steve said.

"Of course."

"Wonderful," Steve said in a funny way. "I knew I could count on you. But I have a better idea."

"Yes . . ."

"*You* walk down the aisle first, and *I'll* be right behind you."

Meanwhile, we had reached the bus stop and were waiting. There were a couple of kids we knew. And Libby, of course. She said to what did she owe the honor of the two of us taking the bus. And then she teased us: "Aren't you afraid of Phil Steinkraus?"

"No!" Steve and I both said together, and Libby laughed.

The bus pulled up and kids started getting on. Steve and I hung back. I wanted Steve in front of me, and he wanted me in front of him. Steve won. I followed Libby onto the bus and Steve was right behind me.

I could see Phil Steinkraus, halfway back in the bus and sitting in an aisle seat. The bad part was that Phil Steinkraus could see me.

153

"Jelly Belly!" he yelled. "Hey! Jelly Belly!"

"Uh oh," Steve said behind me.

Phil Steinkraus was punching every kid who walked past him on the way to the empty seats in the back of the bus. When Libby got to him, however, he left her alone.

There were only a couple of seats between me and Phil Steinkraus now, and no one in the aisle between us. He drew back his arm to punch me. "Come on, Jelly Belly!" he said.

"Who's Jelly Belly?" I said.

"You are."

"He's not fat," Libby said.

"Yes, he is," Phil Steinkraus said.

"Look again, stupid," Libby said.

I drew back my arm like I was going to punch Phil Steinkraus, and I saw him flinch. "There is no Jelly Belly," I said. And I walked on by, daring Phil to punch me.

He didn't. And he didn't punch Steve, either.

And from then on, I never had any more trouble with Phil Steinkraus. But I sometimes wonder to myself . . . what would I have done if he had punched me? Would I have fought back?

And the answer is . . . I don't really know.

It was April. Only a week before we were going off to Disney World. That's when the letter from Richard Napoli came.

Dear Ned,

Guess who got himself even fatter over the winter? Yes, me again.

I got a letter from Hog last week. He's going back to Camp Lean-Too and so is Max. And, unfortunately, so am I. If you are going again, too, I think we could all bunk together. It was fun last Summer.

I have some wonderful ideas of how to stash goodies in your camp trunk so they'll never find it. Write me back and I'll explain. It will work for sure.

Meanwhile, take care and I'll see you in Camp Lean-Too.

Your friend,
Rich

Standing in the front hall, reading Richard's letter, I got this goose-pimply feeling all over. I had almost forgotten about Camp Lean-Too, and the miserable time I had there. The way they starved us. The stolen cheese sandwiches I hated but ate anyway. The candy bar orgies we had out in the woods.

Richard was going back there again. And Hog. And good old Max, from Chicago. All of them were still fat. All of them still had to diet. All of them would spend another stupid summer, fooling themselves in Camp Lean-Too.

I, on the other hand, would never have to go back there again.

ABOUT THE AUTHOR

After a career in advertising, Robert Kimmel Smith turned to writing full time. He has written plays, short stories, and novels such as *Chocolate Fever*, for young people as well as for adults. He lives in Brooklyn, New York.

An experienced dieter, Robert Kimmel Smith considers himself a diet authority, having lost over a thousand pounds in his lifetime.